A magical collection

The bookshelf along the far wall of the Owner's bedroom was lined with jars, top to bottom. To someone who didn't know any better, they would probably look like simple peanut butter jars. All of them unmarked. All of them empty. But the Owner could tell them apart, and they most certainly were not empty.

This was his collection of Talents. Talents for origami and dog-training and computer-repair and whistling, and dozens of others he'd managed to nab over the years. The Owner had always believed that there was really only one Talent you needed in this world: The Talent for appropriating other people's Talents.

Selecting a jar from the back, one which had not yet been filled, the Owner—*swit-tsk-schwap!*—unscrewed the lid. Then he lifted his right hand above the empty jar and squeezed it into a fist. Tighter and tighter he squeezed, until at last . . .

Plunk!

Where just a moment ago there had been nothing, now suddenly there was the Talent the Owner had plucked from the man in the gray suit, clean and condensed and opaque, like an ice cube. The Owner had seen the sight a thousand times, but he never tired of it.

As the Owner reached for the lid to the jar, the Talent began to dissipate, just as the Talents always did if you left them to their own devices. A fine mist rose out of the jar, higher, higher, straight into the air vent above. The Owner thought he heard a soft sniffle escape from the vent, but when he shot his eyes up to check, there was nothing.

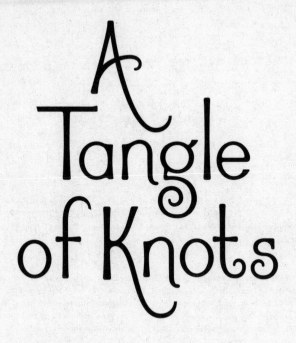

A Tangle of Knots

LISA GRAFF

PUFFIN BOOKS

PUFFIN BOOKS
An imprint of Penguin Random House LLC
375 Hudson Street
New York, New York 10014

First published in the United States of America by Philomel Books,
a division of Penguin Young Readers Group, 2013
Published by Puffin Books, an imprint of Penguin Young Readers Group, 2014

THE LIBRARY OF CONGRESS HAS CATALOGED THE PHILOMEL EDITION AS FOLLOWS:
Graff, Lisa (Lisa Colleen), 1981–.
A tangle of knots / Lisa Graff.
p. cm.
Summary: "Destiny leads 11-year-old Cady to a peanut butter factory, a family of children searching
for their own Talents, and a Talent Thief who will alter her life forever"—Provided by publisher.
Includes cake recipes.
ISBN 978-0-399-25517-5 (hc)
[1. Orphans—Fiction. 2. Baking—Fiction. 3. Ability—Fiction. 4. Identity—Fiction.
5. Family life—New York—Fiction. 6. Poughkeepsie (N.Y.)—Fiction.]
I. Title.
PZ7.G751577Tan 2013
[Fic]—dc23
2012009573

Puffin Books ISBN 9780147510136

Edited by Jill Santopolo.
Design by Amy Wu.
Printed in the United States of America

13 15 17 19 20 18 16 14 12

To Marty,

a classic chocolate cake

(plain, no frosting)

A Tangle
of Knots

Prologue

THE LINE FOR THE NUMBER 36 BUS OUT OF HATTIESBURG, Mississippi, was the longest at the station. All sorts of folks were making the long trip north. There were slouchers and starers. A few snoozers. Puckered here and there along the row were men stretching their limbs, hoping to catch a hint of a breeze. A woman fanned her daughter with a newspaper whose headline read SCIENTISTS BELIEVE EXTINCT JUPITER BIRD MAY HAVE BEEN LARGEST FLYING ANIMAL. A toddler munched a cracker, sprinkling sticky crumbs across his mother's chest. No one seemed to have the energy to speak above a grumble.

The air was thick.

Amidst them all sat a young man, exactly one day past his eighteenth birthday, perched carefully atop his powder blue suitcase. His new brown suit was stiff with creases, not yet shaped to fit his angles. He tapped his foot on the ground, breathing in the last few moments before he claimed his inheritance. His Fate. As soon as he climbed aboard that bus, the young man would be on his way.

Next to him, a small girl who had been losing at a game of jacks for some several minutes suddenly snatched up all seven pieces before the ball bounced down, her hand whipping through the air too quickly to follow.

"Hey!" cried the girl's competitor, a boy at least three years her senior. "No fair! You said you weren't any good at jacks!"

The girl grinned a sly little grin. "I'm not good," she replied, tossing the pieces in the air in a whir of jacks-and-ball-and-jacks. She caught them expertly. "I'm Talented." She pocketed the jacks and held out her hand, where the boy begrudgingly deposited a nickel.

The young man watched as the girl scurried across the line to her mother, who was leafing through a magazine. When the girl proudly produced her nickel, her mother scolded, "Not *again*, Susan." But she only *tsk*ed as her daughter flipped the coin in the air. The young man couldn't help but grin at the scene. *A Talent is only rewarding if you wield it well.* That's what his mother had always told him. It seemed to him that this little girl was a master wielder.

"That's a nice suitcase you've got there."

The young man looked up. Standing before him was a man in a gray suit. He might have been forty, he might have been older, and he was, quite easily, the largest man in the bus station, his enormous frame threatening even the brick support posts for sturdiest structure.

"Sorry?" the young man replied.

"Your suitcase. It's a choice model. Top of the line."

Instinctively, the young man grasped the sides of the suitcase just a little tighter. It was a very old suitcase, but sturdy and well-loved, boxy and large as a small child, with worn corners and three small dimples near the left clasp. Across the top a cursive scrawl of silver thread spelled out the brand: *St. Anthony's*.

Hidden inside the lining was a single slip of paper that constituted the bulk of the young man's inheritance.

The young man cleared his throat. *He's just a friendly traveler,* he told himself, *making conversation.* "Thanks," he replied. "It was my mother's."

The words had slipped out without his meaning them to—*it was*—and he hoped that the older fellow hadn't noticed his use of the past tense. The last thing the young man wanted to talk about was his mother. But the large man in the gray suit merely grinned a sideways sort of grin. It was a grin that suggested he knew more about the world than he was letting on.

As though to thank him for his silence, the young man offered his hand. "Mason Burgess," he introduced himself.

"Pleasure to meet you, Mason," the older fellow replied, leaning down to reach Mason's outstretched hand. The man had a surprisingly firm shake. "Mind if I wait with you?" And with the ease of a man a third his size, he plopped down his worn leather duffel and folded his legs underneath him.

He did not mention his name.

"So," the fellow said to Mason, lifting his hat from his head to wipe his brow. "Going north, are you?"

"Poughkeepsie," Mason confirmed.

"New York," the fellow said, nodding. He seemed not surprised by the information. "Good for you."

"And you?" Mason asked, making conversation.

"I'm a traveling salesman," he replied, although it was most certainly not the answer to Mason's question. "Odds and ends, mostly. I don't suppose I could interest you in a knot?" He opened the right side of his jacket. Inside, where most salesmen might hang watches or whatnots, the old man had pinned dozens and dozens of knots. There were slipknots and topknots and figure eights, and tens more Mason had no name for.

Mason squinted. "You certainly are Talented," he told the man graciously. "Do you . . ." He searched for his manners. ". . . sell many knots, then?"

The older fellow dropped shut the side of his jacket. "Heavens, no," he said, the last of a guffaw trickling over his words. "These are mostly for entertainment. It's a horribly useless

Talent, tying knots. Could have been blessed with a Talent for finance or medicine. Even a log-splitting Talent might have done me some good. But no, I find myself with knot-tying."

"Well, the only knot I've mastered is the one to tie my shoe-laces," Mason admitted. He couldn't help it; he liked the odd fellow. "Every other knot just looks like a tangled mess to me."

The man in the gray suit thought about that. "Well, that's the thing about knots, isn't it?" he replied after a moment. "If you don't know the trick, it's a muddled predicament. But in fact each loop of every knot is carefully placed, one end twisting right into the other in a way you might not have expected. I find them rather beautiful, really."

"Mmm." Mason had nothing more to say on the subject, so he changed course. "It must be an interesting job, traveling salesman," he said. "Seeing the world."

"It isn't bad, at that," the man told him. "I'm saving up for a hot air balloon. Faster travel, and the views are amazing."

Without warning, the bus's engine roared to life. *"Number 36 to Philadelphia!"* the bus driver bellowed. *"Transfer to points north!"* Mason rose to his feet.

"Now, just you remember," the man in the gray suit told Mason, as though they were continuing a previous conversation, "keep an eye on that suitcase of yours."

"Of course I will," Mason snapped, picking the suitcase up by the handle. It weighed less than a loaf of bread. "I don't . . ."

Mason shook his head. *I don't need another father*—that's what he'd begun to say. "I'll be careful," he told the man. "Are you traveling all the way to Philadelphia? Perhaps we might sit next to each other."

The man's gaze was still fixed on Mason's suitcase. "I had one once," he said. "A St. Anthony's suitcase. Did you know there were only three dozen ever crafted? Shut down production after that." He returned his hat to his head and bent to scoop up his duffel. "I let it out of my sight, if you can believe such a thing. Let go of the suitcase for one minute and . . ." He suddenly seemed to notice the line was pressing them forward, and shook his head as he and Mason inched closer to the bus. "Just be sure to keep an eye on it, young man. The St. Anthony's brand, they seem to have a tendency to . . . redistribute themselves."

Mason looked down to discover he was clutching his suitcase close to his chest, like a baby with a rag doll. *Ridiculous.* He lowered his arms, turning from the man in the gray suit just long enough to close the gap in the line.

"I'd be happy to offer you the window seat, if you'd like," Mason said over his shoulder as they continued toward the bus. "Or the aisle, if you'd rather stretch your le—"

Mason stopped talking. Because he had turned around again. And the man in the gray suit was no longer there.

"Suitcase and ticket, please, son."

Mason whirled back around. "Huh?" he muttered to the driver, momentarily confused by his outstretched hand. Where had the large man gone off to? There was no sign of him anywhere.

"Suitcase and ticket, please."

Mason shook himself back to his senses and handed the bus driver his ticket.

"That'll have to go under the bus," the driver told him, pointing to the suitcase in Mason's hand. "No room for it up above."

Mason felt his eyes go wide. "But I . . ." He bit his lip. *You are a grown man now,* he told himself. *Speak with confidence.* "No, thank you, sir. I'd rather keep it with me."

The driver crossed his arms with the impatience of a man too long at his job. "Son, the bus is full, and there's no room for that boxy bag in the overhead. Either you get on board with your suitcase underneath, or both of you stay here. It's up to you." And he reached around Mason's head to grab the ticket of the next passenger in line.

When the bus pulled into the Philadelphia station, Mason Burgess was the first to disembark. He tapped his foot impatiently as the driver unlocked the baggage compartment, then fumbled through the other passengers' bags to find his own.

It was not there.

Mason checked everywhere. He searched the other passengers

as they trotted off with their own suitcases. He crawled inside the baggage compartment to check for hidden nooks and corners. He even threatened the driver. But it was no use.

The suitcase, and the one slim, irreplaceable slip of paper inside it, was gone.

Fifty-Three Years Later . . .

Miss Mallory's Peach Cake

a cake that's sweet, simple, and hard to dislike

FOR THE CAKE:

small sliver of butter (for greasing the cake pan)

3 large eggs, at room temperature

2 cups sliced canned peaches (about 1 ½ 15-ounce cans)

2 cups flour (plus extra for preparing the cake pan)

1 tsp salt

1 tsp baking soda

1 tsp cinnamon

1 ¾ cups granulated sugar

1 cup vegetable oil

½ cup chopped walnuts

FOR THE FROSTING:

3 oz cream cheese, at room temperature

4 tbsp butter, at room temperature

1 tsp vanilla

2 cups powdered sugar

½ tsp ground ginger

1. Preheat oven to 375°F. Grease a 10-inch tube pan or Bundt pan with butter, and flour lightly.

2. In a small bowl, beat the eggs lightly with a fork. Set aside.

3. Drain the canned peaches into a sieve or strainer and rinse them lightly. Pat them dry with a paper towel and measure out 2 cups. Set aside.

4. In a medium bowl, whisk together the flour, salt, baking soda, and cinnamon. Set aside.

5. In a large bowl, mix together the eggs, granulated sugar, and oil with a wooden spoon until just blended. Slowly add the flour mixture and stir until just combined. Carefully fold in the peaches and nuts.

6. Pour the batter into the pan and bake for 50 minutes, or until a toothpick comes out clean. Cool the cake in the pan for 10 minutes, then turn it out onto a cake rack to cool completely before frosting.

7. While the cake is cooling, make the frosting: In a medium bowl, beat the cream cheese, butter, and vanilla with a mixer on medium speed, until well combined and smooth, about 1 to 2 minutes. Reducing the mixer to low speed, gradually add the powdered sugar and ginger, and beat until smooth. Apply frosting to the top of the cooled cake.

Cady

MISS MALLORY'S HOME FOR LOST GIRLS IN POUGHKEEPSIE, New York, was technically an orphanage, but there were hardly ever any orphans there. In fact, most days, if you peeked inside the window, you would see only one orphan, all by herself but hardly lonely, standing on her tiptoes at the kitchen counter, baking a cake.

Cadence, that was her name.

She was standing there now, Cady, deciding what to add to her bowl of batter. If you squinted through the window, you could just make her out from the chin up (Cady was barely a wisp of a thing). You'd see the shiny, crow-black hair that hung smooth as paper from the top of her head to the bottoms of her earlobes. And you'd see the petite—pixieish, Miss Mallory called them—features of her face. Tiny nose, tiny mouth, tiny ears. Cady's eyes, however, those were large in comparison to the rest of her. Large and dark and round, and set just so on a face the color of a leaf that has clung too long to its tree.

Flour, sugar, butter, eggs. Cady studied the bowl in front of her. She closed her eyes, digging into the furthest reaches of her brain to figure out what would be the perfect addition to her cake. At last her thick black lashes fluttered open. She had it.

Cinnamon. She would make a cinnamon cake.

No one knew exactly when Cady's Talent for baking had first emerged—just as no one knew exactly where she had come from. But one thing was certain: Cady was a Talented baker. She could bake anything, really. Pies. Muffins. Bread. Casseroles. Even the perfect pizza if she put her mind to it. But what Cady loved above all else was baking cakes. All she needed to do was to close her eyes, and she could imagine the absolutely perfect cake for any person, anywhere. A pinch more salt, a touch less cream. It was one hundred percent certain that the person she was baking for would never have tasted anything quite so heavenly in all his life. In fact, what the orphanage lacked in orphans it made up for in cake-baking trophies. Five first-place trophies from the Sunshine Bakers of America Annual Cake Bakeoff lined the front hall, one for every year that Cady had entered from the age of five, when her oven mitts swallowed her up to the elbows. No matter who entered the competition—professional bakers, famous chefs with exclusive restaurants—none of their Talents were able to match Cady's, not for five years running. Cady's cakes were never the most beautiful, or the most stunning. Last year not one but two bakers had crafted fifty-layer-high masterpieces of sugary wonder, studded with frosted stars and flowers and figurines. One even included a working chocolate fountain. Cady's single-layer pistachio sheet cake had looked pitiful in comparison. But nonetheless, it had been the judge's favorite, because Cady had baked it specifically for him.

This year's bakeoff would be held in just one short week in New York City, a two-hour drive away. Miss Mallory had already cleared space in the hallway for a sixth trophy.

The kitchen door squeaked open and in waltzed Miss Mallory, a polka-dot tablecloth folded in her arms. (Miss Mallory's perfect cake, as far as Cady was concerned, was just as scrumptious as she was—a nutty peach cake with cream cheese frosting.)

"What did you come up with?" Miss Mallory asked, crossing the room to peer into the cake bowl.

Cady found the cinnamon in the cabinet above her and popped off the lid. "Cinnamon," she replied, shaking the spice into the bowl. Cady had no need for measurements. "A cinnamon cake, three layers high."

Miss Mallory took a deep breath of pleasure. "And the frosting?"

Cady did not even need a moment to think. She *knew* the answer, sensed it the way other people could sense which way to walk home after a stroll in the woods. "Chocolate buttercream with a hint of spice," she replied.

"Perfect," Miss Mallory said. "Amy will love it." She snuck a finger out from under her tablecloth to poke a tiny glob from the bowl. "I hope this fog finally gives up," she said, sighing as the taste of the batter hit her tongue.

Cady had been so intent on her baking that she hadn't even noticed the haze. She peered out the window. Out on the lawn, the thick mist obscured all but the legs of the picnic table, and puddles speckled the steps to the porch.

It had been foggy the morning Cady was brought to Miss Mallory's, too. Cady had been much too young to remember it, but she'd heard the story so many times that the details were as real and comfortable as a pair of well-worn shoes. The damp smell of the dew outside. The mystery novel Miss Mallory had been reading when she heard the knock at the door. And most especially, Miss Mallory's surprise at the arrival.

"I'd never seen a baby so small," Miss Mallory always told her. "And with such a remarkable head of hair. There was a braid woven into it." Here Miss Mallory would trace the plaits across Cady's scalp, making Cady's skin tingle delightfully. "It was the most intricate braid I've ever seen, twisted in and about and around itself like a crown. Whoever gave you that braid was Talented indeed."

Miss Mallory snuck one more fingerful of batter from the bowl. "Perhaps we should move the party inside today," she suggested.

"But Adoption Day parties are *always* outside," Cady protested, slapping Miss Mallory's hand away playfully. There wasn't much consistency in the life of an orphan—new housemates coming and going like waves on a shore—but Adoption Day parties were always the same. Adoption Day parties took place outside, with presents and card games (it was difficult to play other sorts of games with so few people about) and a cake baked by Cady for the lucky little girl whose Adoption Day it was.

People sometimes suspected, when they learned how few orphans lived at Miss Mallory's Home for Lost Girls, that it must be a sorry excuse for an orphanage. But the truth was quite the opposite. The truth was that most of the orphans at Miss Mallory's found their perfect families astonishingly quickly. Miss Mallory had a Talent for matching orphans to families—she felt a tug, deep in her chest, she said, when she sensed that two people truly belonged together, and she just knew. Most of the little girls who came through the orphanage doors were matched within days of arriving, sometimes hours. Miss Mallory had famously matched one girl only seven minutes after she stepped off her train. They would send photos, those lucky little girls who had found their perfect families, and Miss Mallory would frame them and hang them in the front hallway, just above Cady's row of trophies. Smiling kids, beaming parents.

Cady had studied them carefully.

Cady was the only orphan at Miss Mallory's who had ever stayed for an extended period of time. Oh, Miss Mallory had tried to match her. Over the years Cady had been sent to live with no fewer than six families—loving, happy, wonderful families—but unlike with the other orphans, it had never quite worked out. Cady had always done her best to be the perfect daughter. She *yes, ma'am*ed and *no, sir*ed and ate all her vegetables and went to bed on time. But no fewer than six times, Miss Mallory had come to return Cady to the orphanage long before her one-week trial period was over. "I made a mistake," Miss Mallory always told her. "That wasn't your perfect family."

But Cady knew that Miss Mallory didn't make mistakes. Somehow, for some reason that Cady couldn't explain, the fault lay with her. And Cady vowed that if she ever got another chance, with another family, she would do whatever it took to make it work. One day she would have an Adoption Day party of her own. One day she would bake the perfect cake for herself.

"Maybe," Cady said slowly, glancing outside at the beautifully foggy morning, "maybe today's the day I'll meet my family." The very idea warmed her through just as much as the heat from the oven. She tugged an oven mitt onto each hand and opened the oven door, then set the cake pans on the center rack. "Maybe," she said again, "my real and true family will step right out of the fog."

The Owner

IT WAS AN UNUSUALLY FOGGY MORNING, SO MURKY THAT THE Owner of the Lost Luggage Emporium at 1 Argyle Road in Poughkeepsie, New York, could scarcely see the ground in front of him. But the Owner had very little use for ground these days.

He tapped his toes at the air, two inches above the soggy soil, as he finished affixing the sign to the Emporium's door.

ROOMS FOR RENT
CHEAP RATES!

The Owner (that's what they called him around town, ever since he'd opened up the Emporium, and it was how he'd come to think of himself, too) was not thrilled at the idea of renting out the building's empty upstairs bedrooms. But a hard look at his finances had finally convinced him that he had no other choice. Although his mother had amassed quite a fortune—an especially impressive feat for a woman with no Talent—it hadn't been enough to last him fifty-three years.

The telltale sound of tires starting down the long wooded stretch of Argyle Road sent the Owner floating back inside the building. It couldn't be Toby already—the dolt had only just left for the morning's luggage pickup an hour ago. The door slammed shut behind him with a crooked *wha-pop!* One more thing the Owner couldn't afford to fix.

The building had once been an architectural beauty, as famous for its two tall, round turrets as for the goods that were produced inside. Now, its white paint was peeling, its shutters were cracked, its windows were grimy with dust. As old and bleak as its owner, that's what Toby liked to say.

The Owner reached the circular wooden counter at the center of the main storeroom and lifted the hinged section to float inside, settling himself behind the register. A hastily hand-lettered green sign hung above the countertop, displaying the store's motto:

LOST LUGGAGE EMPORIUM
DISCOVER WHAT EVERYONE ELSE IS MISSING

"This is quite the setup you've got here," the customer called as he entered the store. Tendrils of fog curled their way in behind him before the door had a chance to close. *Wha-pop!* The customer jerked his head on his spindly neck, indicating the various sections of the store—the racks of clothing, the shelves of books, the electronics, the appliances, and, of course, the suitcases. "All this stuff really come from lost luggage?"

The Owner did not look up from his book. It was the latest Victoria Valence mystery, *Face Value*, and it really was quite good (although it wouldn't have mattered if it weren't). "Mmm," he replied.

"Nice Talent you got, too." The customer flicked a hand toward the Owner's legs, exposed beneath the hinged section of the countertop. "Floating, huh? Been a while since I saw a Talent like that."

The Owner stopped his toe-tapping just long enough to nudge a powder blue suitcase farther under the countertop. "It keeps the mud off my shoes," he muttered, turning a page in his book.

"Keeps the mud off your shoes!" The man hooted. "That's a riot." He shook his head, grinning like an imbecile. "Wish I had a Talent that good. All I got's whistling." And he puckered his lips and began to whistle a happy little ditty, right there in the store.

Finally he wandered off to peruse the merchandise.

He returned much too quickly for the Owner's taste, however (still whistling, unfortunately). "Ring me up!" the customer cried cheerfully, placing two worn leather bags and a winter jacket on the counter.

As the man dug for his wallet, the Owner, quietly and stealthily, slipped his right hand into his own pocket to find the small glass jar he always kept ready for a ripe opportunity. With practiced ease, he unscrewed the lid. Then he squeezed his hand into a fist. His palm grew icier and icier, until—*plunk!*—an almost imperceptible whisper of a noise escaped from the jar, and the Owner's feet dropped—*clonk!*—to the ground. The customer was too busy stuffing his items into a plastic bag to notice.

The Owner removed his hand from his pocket, just as he'd done so many times before, and stretched it across the counter. "I appreciate your business," the Owner told him. The customer suspected nothing. None of them ever suspected.

They shook.

"Ooh!" the customer cried suddenly. He rubbed his fingers. "Cold hands."

"Really?" The Owner's attention turned back to his novel. "Must be my poor circulation." And he didn't raise his eyes again until the customer reached the front door, where he (still not suspecting a thing) puckered his lips to whistle.

But, of course, all that came out was a weak cough.

When the sound of the man's car had at last receded down

the long stretch of Argyle Road, the Owner clasped and unclasped his icy fingers, the way a child might test out a toy he hadn't played with in some time.

Then, pursing together his lips, the Owner began to whistle.

There were eight bedrooms on the second floor of the Lost Luggage Emporium. On that foggy Friday morning, six of them were available for rent.

The Owner didn't know it then, but in just one short week, all eight rooms would be filled. Some would be occupied by people with great Talents, others would not. One would house a thief, a person in possession of an object worth millions of dollars. Several would be inhabited by liars. But every last person would have something in common.

In just one short week, every last one of them would have lost the thing they treasured most in the world.

Marigold

MARIGOLD ASHER TWISTED HER RED TALENT BRACELET around and around her wrist. It was the thing she treasured most in the world, because it was the thing that was finally going to help her discover her Talent. This was the day, she could feel it. Anything could happen on a foggy morning.

Marigold studied the nearly finished goldfish piñata on the kitchen table before her. Just one more piece of tissue paper and it would be complete. She dabbed a thin leaf of black tissue with glue and . . .

Tipped over the glue bottle. Marigold grabbed for it, but knocked over a teetering stack of tissue paper instead. She lunged for *that*, but whacked the piñata. The goldfish crashed to the floor. It broke in two. With a sinking stomach, Marigold watched its severed head roll, roll, roll across the kitchen.

Your piñata skills need work, its gaping fish mouth seemed to tell her.

"Where's Mom?" asked Marigold's younger brother, Will, appearing from nowhere (Will was always appearing from nowhere). He plowed across the tissue paper battlefield, his shoes collecting colorful scraps. His pet ferret, Sally, was right behind him, snatching up small bits of paper in her teeth and sniffing them before spitting them out again.

Marigold snatched her sticky pencil from the table and crossed *piñata making* off her list of possible Talents. "Mom has the hospital this morning, remember?" Every few weeks their mother dropped off a load of scarves and blankets for patients at the Poughkeepsie Medical Center. She knitted most of the objects on her way, clasping her knitting needles around the steering wheel as she drove. Mrs. Asher's Talent for knitting was so keen that she could finish an entire afghan in eight city blocks.

Will scooped Sally off the floor and settled her on his shoulder. "You tried all these Talents this morning?" he asked Marigold, studying her list on the table.

"Yep." Marigold gathered her brown curls off her shoulders and counted off in her head. "Running backward, making applesauce, doing jumping jacks, gargling, blowing bubbles, slicing garlic, making a house out of playing cards, stringing popcorn, organizing furniture, drawing mazes, and making piñatas."

"Wow."

"Dad even convinced me my Talent might be vacuuming," she told her brother, scraping a bit of orange tissue off the table-top as she spoke. "He got me to do the whole living room before he left for the grocery store." Mr. Asher was the head librarian at the local high school, so he had summers off. (He also had an unusual—if not particularly useful—Talent. While most people in the world could fold a sheet of paper in half no more than seven times, Mr. Asher could do it twelve. It was a trick he'd often perform for school groups, if someone brought him a bit of orange nougat. Mr. Asher had a soft spot for orange nougat.)

"Don't worry, Mari," Will said, scratching Sally's belly. She clicked a few satisfied *click-click-clacks*, then wrapped herself around his neck, settling into a quiet snore. A sleepy scarf. "You'll find it."

Marigold grabbed a damp dish towel from the edge of the sink to better scrub at the tabletop. "Thanks, Will. Maybe next I should try something a little less mess—" Marigold looked up. "Will?"

Her brother was gone.

It wasn't an uncommon occurrence, Will going missing. He had a Talent for it, after all. Even in the cramped space of their twelfth-story apartment, Will managed to get lost at least once an hour. Sometimes he popped right out of the woodwork after only a second, and other times it might take all day to find him.

"Zane!" Marigold called to her other brother, marching toward the living room with the dish towel clutched at her side. "Will's missing agai—"

She saw it coming just in time—the arc of spit heading down the hallway, straight toward her. Marigold shrieked, covering her face with the dish towel. The glob of spit zoomed— *slurrrrrp!*—over her head.

"Zane!" she hollered. He was sitting, calm and smug as ever, in the armchair by the window, reading a book. Under his feet was his trusty skateboard, rolling a few inches this way, then that. Zane was the only Asher without a jumble of brown curls on top of his head. He wore his hair in short, pointy spikes. Marigold often wondered if it would be possible to smooth out her brother's prickly personality just by chopping off that hair.

"Mom said if you ever spit at me again, she'll—"

"I didn't spit *at* you," Zane replied, barely lifting his eyes from his book. "I spit *over* you. If I wanted to spit *at* you, I would've hit you."

Marigold huffed, but she knew he was right. That someone as annoying as Zane Asher had been given the Talent of perfect spitting was truly unconscionable. "Well . . ." She searched for something to blame him for. Her eyes landed on the red Talent bracelet around her wrist, now sticky with glue-water from its run-in with the dish towel. "You got my bracelet all gunky."

Zane shrugged, eyes still on his book. Out the open window behind him, a thick blanket of fog rolled peacefully across the sky. "I can't believe you think something you got out of a gumball machine will actually help you find your Talent," he said.

"I did *not* get it out of a gumball machine," Marigold growled. "For your information, I got it at the state fair last week, and the man said it had a ninety-nine percent success rate for helping people discover their Talents within one year." She rubbed the stickiness out on the edge of her T-shirt. "It cost three whole months' allowance."

Zane turned a page in his book. "You'd have better luck with a gumball," he replied.

Some kids had older brothers who were friendly, Marigold thought. Supportive, even. "I'm going to tell Mom and Dad you spit at me," she retorted. But she knew it was useless, like a poodle puppy yipping at a full-grown rottweiler.

"If you do that," Zane told her, the skateboard whirring under his feet as his eyes scanned his book, not even the least distracted, "I'll tell them you haven't practiced oboe in a week."

Marigold fought the urge to stick her tongue out at him. She wound her bracelet around her wrist again, fingering the knotted red thread, the three sparkly silver beads. Ten years old and no Talent, that was Marigold Asher. No one in the Asher family could possibly understand what it was like to still be searching, to constantly worry that you might be Fair. After all, weren't the majority of the people in the world without any Talent middle children, just like Marigold? Middlings, that's what they called them.

Well, *she* wasn't. Marigold had a Talent hidden somewhere deep inside her, she was sure of it. All she needed to do was find it. So what was the use in wasting time at something you knew you stunk at—like practicing the oboe—when you could be discovering your one true Talent?

"I'm going to look for Will," Marigold said, shooting Zane a final glare as she left the room. "Try not to kill anyone, all right?"

If only she had known what a wise warning that would turn out to be.

V

FOR A SINGLE BRIEF SECOND, SHE'D THOUGHT SHE'D DIED.
Total blackness, total silence, swallowed by nothingness. And all
she could think was, *Caroline*. If she were dead, she could see
her daughter. Talk to her again.

But she was not, as it turned out, dead.

When she came to, she was lying on her back in the middle
of the highway. There were people looming over her—four of
them, a woman and three men, strangers all—peering down,
blinking, looking concerned. And there were cars stopped still
in the street. The red and blue lights of a police car whirred in
circles. She could just barely make it all out through the thicket
of fog.

But what was truly unnerving was that the people around her were not speaking any language she'd ever heard before. When they opened their mouths, the noise that came out wasn't words. It was the clamor of bees buzzing, or horns honking, or waves crashing against the shore. Not a language at all.

English, she tried to tell them. *Speak English.*

But what she spoke wasn't English, either. It certainly wasn't words. She could hear the noise, with her own perfectly functioning ears, escaping her perfectly functioning mouth. She was speaking gibberish, too.

A stroke. She'd had a stroke. It was her *brain* that wasn't functioning properly. She'd spent the majority of her sixty years cooped up in her house, and then the day after her doctor told her she better start getting more exercise—for her health, he said—that's when she went and had herself a stroke crossing the wooded highway. And now she'd lost her words.

One of the men was bending down, pointing to his driver's license, a question painted on his face. Her name. They wanted to know her name.

She did not have any real identification. (Who carried identification when they were off for a short, pleasant stroll in the woods?) So, by way of an answer, she showed them the locket. The silver one she wore around her neck. There was no picture inside, not anymore, not since her Caroline had left, but there was one clue etched on the outside. She could see it herself with her perfectly functioning eyes, although she found it difficult to read (she supposed she had lost that, too—reading): two straight lines inscribed in the center of the silver oval, meeting at a sharp point.

V

The man bent down and inspected the locket, grasping it between thick fingers. She waited, holding her breath, to see if perhaps he was Talented at solving mysteries. But he only looked up at the others and shook his head, confused.

They did not know who she was. Perhaps if she found a map somehow, she could show them where she lived. Or if there was a book she could get her hands on, she might . . . She squeezed shut her eyes as they lifted her onto the gurney. What was the point? First she'd lost Caroline and now, her words. And without those two most precious things, there really was no point to much of anything at all.

Zane

NORMALLY ZANE WASN'T MUCH FOR WORDS ON A PAGE. HE'D rather be skateboarding, or spitting, or sticking gum on the floor 9 elevator button so that cranky Mr. Watkins had something to give him the stink eye *for*. But Zane's father always said that reading a good book helped take your mind off your problems, so here Zane was. Reading. *Face Value*, that was the book, a mystery novel by Victoria Valence. He'd found it in his mother's knitting basket.

It wasn't helping.

WORTHLESS.

That was the noise Zane heard as he turned the page. He pressed it flat and did his best to focus.

The plot was interesting, at least, about a rogue treasure hunter with a Talent for changing his face—a chameleon, he was called. Right now he was posing as the Egyptian detective assigned to gather information about the museum heist the chameleon himself had pulled off in the first chapter. (As sneaky and shifty as the chameleon was, he had a charm about him that people couldn't seem to resist.) Juicy stuff, and yet Zane couldn't keep his mind from wandering.

WORTHLESS.

It might be nice, Zane thought, to be able to change your face whenever you wanted, to start fresh, just like that. And if the stupid principal ever sent a stupid letter to your parents, you could just slap on a new face and no one would even know it was you the letter was about.

WORTHLESS, Zane Asher, that's what you are. A delinquent. A waste of a perfectly good desk. I'll be writing to your parents and letting them know as much. If you come back to this school again next year, God help me, Zane Asher, it won't be me who has the problem.

Zane tossed the book across the room. What did Principal Piles know, anyway? That old bat was the one who ought to be sent to boarding school.

He turned his attention to the fog out the window and aimed a spit attack at an unsuspecting pigeon passing by the fire escape. *Ptew!* Right in the beak. Spitting was one thing Zane never failed at. If only he could spit that letter right out of the mailbox.

WORTHLESS.

Until he could grow a Talent for making mail disappear, Zane decided he should probably work on a good lie to tell his parents when they actually did open the mail. Because sooner or later, that stupid letter was going to arrive, and if Zane didn't have a plan, he was done for.

6

Miss Mallory

"Cady! The mail's here!"

Jennifer Mallory hadn't noticed the mailman arriving through the fog, but nevertheless the mailbox was full. She clicked shut the mailbox door and headed through the damp gray air to the picnic table by the front door, settled between the carefully groomed bed of petunias on the left and the meticulously weeded pansies on the right.

"Here's one from the Sunshine Bakeoff," Miss Mallory told Cady, who was busy making preparations for the party. Little Amy would be arriving with her new parents any moment. Miss Mallory pulled the thick envelope from the stack.

"The tickets!" Cady squealed. And sure enough, there were three tickets inside, just the same as there were every year. One ticket for the baker, and two for her guests. (Since there was never anyone at the orphanage who stuck around long enough to attend special events, it had always only been the two of them—Miss Mallory and Cady—attending every year. Which meant that every year, one of the guest tickets remained, unused, inside its envelope.) "You don't mind going again this year, do you, Miss Mallory?" Cady asked in that shy, thoughtful way of hers. "It must get awfully boring sitting there, watching cakes bake."

Miss Mallory put a hand to her chest, where an unwelcome tug had been growing all morning. She had a sinking suspicion that sooner rather than later there wouldn't be an extra ticket left in that envelope at all. If Miss Mallory was correct about the tug in her chest (and she worried that this time she was), Cady's perfect family was right around the corner.

"There's nothing I'd rather do in the world than watch you knock everybody's socks off with one of your cakes," she told Cady truthfully. Cady smiled her shy little smile. "I'll come to watch you bake as long as you'll keep inviting me."

"You know I'll always invite you," Cady replied. "Every single year." The tug in Miss Mallory's chest jerked a little harder, but she said nothing.

While Cady strolled back to the table to straighten out the polka-dot cloth, Miss Mallory stuck her nose inside the Sunshine Bakers information packet.

"There's a change to the judging procedures," she told Cady, crossing the fog to read to her. "'This year, for the first t

Sunshine Bakers of America Annual Cake Bakeoff

judged by not one but—'"

Without warning, Cady snapped her head up from the table. "My cake's ready!" she announced, as though a buzzer had gone off in the kitchen. But of course, there had been no buzzer. Cady seemed to be able to sense things about her cakes, deep in her bones, the way Miss Mallory could with her orphans.

Cady dashed off into the empty orphanage.

Eleven years ago, the orphanage's upstairs rooms had been practically bursting with girls. Girls giggling, girls fighting, girls making messes. Miss Mallory had never been happier. But as she grew more accustomed to her Talent, Miss Mallory had become faster and faster at matching orphans, and these days, she felt lucky if a girl stayed with her for a handful of hours. Day in and day out, the only constant Miss Mallory had come to count on was Cady.

Precious Cady.

From the instant Miss Mallory had held the sprite of a child to her chest on that foggy morning eleven years ago, she'd known the girl was special. The tiny little thing had wrapped her arms around Miss Mallory's neck and shaped her body into Miss Mallory's curves. And all at once, it had become clear to Miss Mallory that the child's heartbeat matched up precisely with her own. *Tra-thump. Tra-thump. Tra-thump.* They were beating in time together, a perfect rhythm.

Miss Mallory had named the girl Cadence.

"Who braided her hair?" Miss Mallory had asked, marveling at the intricate, almost unearthly weave in the girl's remarkable head of fine black hair.

"It's been like that since we took her on," the couple who brought her told Miss Mallory. "We don't know much about the girl, quite honestly. Between a batch of misfiled paperwork and a fire at her previous orphanage, we're not sure if she was picked up one week ago or twenty, down the block or halfway across the world."

The foggy air grew rich with the scent of cinnamon as Cady pulled her cakes from the oven. Miss Mallory breathed it in, deep and deeper, trying her best to quiet the ever-insistent tug in her chest. She straightened the corners of the polka-dot cloth. Today was an Adoption Day, she reminded herself. A happy celebration. And the future, well, that was still unknown.

Mrs. Asher

DOLORES ASHER GLANCED AT THE CHART THE ATTENDING doctor had just placed at the foot of the newest patient's bed.

Name: UNKNOWN
Age: UNKNOWN
Talent: UNKNOWN
Gender: FEMALE

"Isn't that just the saddest thing?" a nurse asked, noticing Dolores's gaze. "She had a stroke, poor dear, and can't speak a word. She won't even have a place to stay when she gets out of here, if no family or friends come to claim her."

Dolores plucked a cozy purple shawl from the pile of knits she'd brought in. "May I?" she asked the nurse, then reached to drape the shawl across the patient's shoulders. The woman was lost in a fretful sleep. *What a lot of stories she must have to tell*, Dolores thought, *and who knows if she'll ever be able to tell them?*

"Oh, careful there, honey," the nurse exclaimed, throwing a protective arm over Dolores's head to block her from a nearby IV stand. Dolores heard a soft *clack* as something dropped to the floor. "Your hairpin," the nurse told her, snatching up the object.

"Thank you so much," Dolores replied, taking the hairpin from the nurse. She whisked her limp brown curls off her shoulders and wound them quickly into a bun, exactly the way she'd done every morning for the past eleven years. "I don't know what I'd do if I lost this thing." She pierced her mound of hair with the pointier end of the hairpin. It was an unusual piece of decoration, that was for sure—beige and cracked and knobby, as wide as a rib of celery and as long as a pencil. ("It looks like someone dug it out of the *dirt!*" Will had once exclaimed. And indeed it did.)

"Thanks again for the blankets and things," the nurse told her. "You're so lucky to have a Talent you enjoy. Could've been stuck with plant-watering like me." She laughed.

Dolores nodded and smiled, because it was the sort of thing a person nodded and smiled at. But the truth was, there were times Dolores didn't feel quite so lucky. There were times when she found herself thinking longingly of the days before three kids and her own yarn shop, when she'd worked at the Pough-keepsie Museum of Natural Sciences on a scholarship for Fair students. Dolores adjusted her hairpin slightly and glanced at the woman's chart again.

Talent: UNKNOWN

Sometimes that didn't seem so terrible.

As Dolores slid into her car, she spied the papers strewn across the passenger's seat, the mail she'd grabbed from the box on her way out of the apartment. There was one envelope that seemed to be screaming to be opened. MCDERMOTT ELEMENTARY SCHOOL, printed in the upper left corner in fat red letters. Dolores had a sinking suspicion that whatever was in that envelope was not going to make her happy.

Dolores slammed her door shut. Best to head home and worry about unpleasant letters later. She'd been away long enough, and there was a good chance that Will was lost in the apartment walls by now.

She drove off into the fog.

Will's S'more Cake

a cake that always disappears quickly

FOR THE CAKE:

small spoonful of flour, for preparing the cake pan

14-oz package of graham crackers (about 26 crackers)

2 tsp baking powder

1 cup butter (2 sticks), at room temperature
(plus extra for greasing the cake pan)

2 cups granulated sugar

5 large eggs, at room temperature

2 tsp vanilla

1 cup milk, at room temperature

FOR THE FROSTING:

1 cup semisweet chocolate chips

3/4 cup butter (1 1/2 sticks), at room temperature

1 1/2 cups powdered sugar

1/3 cup sour cream, at room temperature

pinch of salt

FOR THE FILLING:

1 cup marshmallow fluff

FOR THE TOPPING:

extra graham crackers and/or mini marshmallows (optional)

1. Preheat oven to 350°F. Lightly grease the bottoms of two 8-inch round cake pans with butter. Using the cake pans as a template, trace two circles onto wax paper and cut them out, placing one wax circle in the bottom of each pan. Grease both pans with butter again, covering the wax paper as well as the sides of the pan. Sprinkle the inside of the pans lightly with flour, and tap the pans to distribute it evenly.

2. Place graham crackers in a blender or food processor, and grind until crushed to a fine powder. (Alternatively, place the graham crackers in a plastic ziplock bag and crush them with a rolling pin.) Measure out 3 cups of the graham cracker powder into a medium bowl, and mix with the baking powder. Set aside. Reserve the remaining graham cracker powder to decorate the top of the cake, if desired.

3. In a large bowl, cream the butter and granulated sugar with an electric mixer, starting on low speed then increasing to medium-high, until light and fluffy, about 3 to 5 minutes. Add the eggs, one at a time, beating well after each addition. Blend in the vanilla.

4. Reducing the speed on the mixer to low, add about a third of the graham cracker mixture to the batter, combining well. Add about half of the milk and combine. Then add another third of the graham cracker mixture, the last of the milk, and then the last of the graham crackers, combining well each time.

5. Pour the batter into the two pans, smoothing the surface. Bake for 35 to 40 minutes, or until a toothpick comes out clean. Let the cakes cool completely before frosting.

6. While the cakes are baking, make the frosting: In a double boiler or a heatproof bowl fitted into a saucepan of simmering water, carefully melt the chocolate chips over low heat, stirring often. Remove from heat and allow to cool, about 10 to 15 minutes.

7. In a large bowl, cream the butter with an electric mixer fitted with clean beaters on medium speed until fluffy, about 2 to 3 minutes. Reducing the speed on the mixer to low, gradually add the powdered sugar and beat until smooth, another 2 to 3 minutes. Add the cooled chocolate, sour cream, and pinch of salt, and beat to combine.

8. When the cakes are completely cooled, place one cake layer on a plate and spread marshmallow fluff on top. (If fluff is difficult to spread, microwave it in a microwave-safe bowl for 10 to 20 seconds and stir.) Place the second cake layer on top and frost the whole cake with chocolate frosting. Decorate with graham crackers, cracker crumbs, or mini marshmallows as desired.

Will

Will's mother liked to say that Will had a Talent for getting lost. But in all his six years, Willard Asher had never once been lost. How could he be lost when he always knew exactly where he was?

At that very moment, for example, Will was inside the walls of the Ashers' apartment building, navigating with the help of an outmoded dumbwaiter that probably no one but him knew existed anymore.

"Today's the day," he told his ferret, Sally, as he tugged at the dumbwaiter's chain, hand over hand, pulling the two of them slowly down through the walls of the building. He was always careful to keep a close eye on Sally when they went exploring.

She had an unfortunate habit of running off, usually to hide something shiny she'd discovered. Sally loved to hide shiny things. "We're going to find an adventure today, I just know it."

In reply, Sally snuggled tighter against his neck and chattered out a *click-click-clack*.

Will and Sally searched for adventure together nearly every day. They knew exactly what adventure looked like because of the storybooks Will read. Giants. Monsters. Cake. That was what the knights in the storybooks always found on their adventures.

Well, Will had added the cake part himself, but it really *did* belong in any good adventure.

Will pulled himself all the way down to the first floor, then all the way back up to the twelfth. He passed Mrs. Castillo's apartment on the eleventh floor, heard her brushing her teeth. He passed the Sansonis on floor ten, listened awhile to the game show they were watching on TV. And he passed old Mr. Watkins on the ninth floor, heard him hollering about gum in the elevator. At every stop, Will nudged his face into the cracks of the mostly plastered-up wall to see what he could see.

No adventure.

Slowly, Will made his way back to the twelfth floor and squeezed out from behind the wardrobe in Marigold's bedroom.

That was when he heard the noise. Although it was less of a

noise and more of a flip-you-on-your-head-pound-your-pancreas-to-pudding sort of *tumult*. The crash shook the whole floor, the whole apartment. It had come from the living room, where Zane had been reading.

Will and Sally reached the living room at the same moment as Marigold. "What was that *noise*?" she asked. "What happ—"

At first Will didn't understand what could possibly make his sister freeze in the middle of a sentence like that. At first, all Will noticed was Zane, sitting silently in the armchair, his face white with terror, his eyes round and unblinking.

And then, of course, Will noticed the rest of it.

Where just minutes earlier there had been a living room wall with a wide window, now there was nothing. Only swirls of fog. Zane sat before the enormous gaping hole, clutching the chair's armrests so tightly, his knuckles were purple. A small black bird flew past and, just for a moment, nipped at the knitted doily on the back of Zane's chair.

Sally hopped down from Will's shoulder and scurried across the floor to the edge where the wall had been. "Sally!" Will cried as he followed her, picking his way across the rubble. "Careful!" He scooped her up.

"What *happened*?" This time Marigold managed to get out a full sentence.

Will dropped to his belly for a closer look, his nose dangling over the edge as he gazed down, down, down into the fog. "It looks like . . ." he said slowly, not quite sure he believed his own eyes, ". . . a hot air balloon."

Click-click-clack. Sally seemed to agree. It *was* a hot air balloon, smashed to bits on the sidewalk twelve stories below. The basket was crumbled, the red-and-blue striped bag ripped and deflated. The passengers were nowhere to be seen. Cars were honking, a passerby with a ruined bag of groceries was cursing at the sky. But as far as Will could make out, nothing had been damaged besides the Ashers' living room wall.

It wasn't quite an adventure, but it sure was *something*.

Toby

SOMETHING HAD HAPPENED ON THE HIGHWAY, THAT'S WHAT they were saying on the radio. A hiker had fainted or fallen or some such thing, which had caused several fender benders, backing up traffic for miles. Which was why Toby now found himself turning unfamiliar corners in the fog.

Toby had been making the same run to the airport every day for over a decade, purchasing the cast-off luggage that no one had come to claim so that the contents might be resold at the Emporium. And every one of those days, from dawn to dusk, had been more or less the same. Far from grand but not too horrible, either, like a pebble underneath your sock that's not quite large enough to bother removing.

Today, it seemed, was different. Toby had never had such a huge haul from an airport run before. And there had even been one of those old powder blue suitcases, a St. Anthony's, which ought to make the old man happy. (*That would be a sight,* Toby thought to himself.) Toby had settled the St. Anthony's next to him in the passenger's seat of his truck for safekeeping.

And that's where it should have stayed, except that, while Toby was turning another corner into the gray fog, the suitcase tumbled to the floor of the truck. Toby reached over to tug it back onto the seat, his eyes drifting from the road for just one moment.

Which, as it happened, was just long enough.

Toby slammed on his brakes. Standing not ten inches from his front bumper was a pixie of a girl with crow-black hair. In her hand was a plate of cake, her fork frozen halfway to her face as she stared at Toby through the windshield. A young woman, tall and thin, rushed over and grabbed the girl by the shoulders. "Cady!" she cried. "Are you okay?"

Toby was parked in the middle of a damp green lawn. Another little girl, much younger than the first, sat in front of a deck of cards at a picnic table covered with a polka-dot cloth, a friendly looking couple beside her. In the distance, Toby could just make out the hazy outline of the sign on the lawn's edge.

MISS MALLORY'S HOME FOR LOST GIRLS

"I'm . . . I'm fine," the girl told the woman, who must have been Miss Mallory herself. "I . . ." The girl blinked. "He just appeared." With the tines of her fork she gestured to Toby through the windshield. "Right out of the fog."

Toby felt his face flush as he studied the girl standing before him. Could it possibly . . . ? He shook his head clear of wild thoughts, quickly unbuckled his seat belt, and leapt from the truck. "I'm so sorry," he said. "I don't know what happened."

When Miss Mallory first opened her mouth to respond, Toby was certain she was going to shout at him, and he wouldn't have blamed her. But to his surprise, she seemed to change her mind. With one hand clutched to her chest, she gave him a sharp nod.

"Would you like to join us for some cake?" she asked, taking the black-haired girl's hand in her own. "We'd be happy to have you."

"I . . ." Toby began, his head turned halfway toward his truck. The engine was still running. "I don't know if I . . ."

"Oh, please do!" the girl—Cady—said. "I made the cake myself. It's delicious."

And at that, Toby smiled. It was a real and true smile, the kind he hadn't felt in a long, long time. "Of course I will," he replied. He turned off his truck and took a seat at the picnic table near the front door, nestled between a bed of petunias on the left and a bed of pansies on the right. Miss Mallory handed him a plate of cake. Each crumb looked moist and rich and heavenly. "I'm Jennifer Mallory," she introduced herself.

"Toby Darlington," he replied.

Which was only partly a lie.

"Do you have a Talent?" the younger girl asked him from the far end of the table. "Mine's licking envelopes. I can do twenty in eight seconds, no paper cuts."

"Amy, dear, don't talk with your mouth full," the woman who must have been Amy's mother admonished. "And we don't ask people about their Talents. It's rude."

"It's okay," Toby replied. "I don't have a Talent," he told Amy. "I'm Fair."

Which was absolutely a lie.

Across the table, Toby noticed Cady studying him carefully. He felt for a moment that she was looking right through him, right to the very depths of who he was. Toby wasn't entirely certain that anyone had ever looked at him that way before. "Is everything all right?" he asked her kindly, raising the fork to his mouth.

"Oh, I was just trying to see what kind of cake you are," Cady replied, offering an embarrassed little grin before taking a small nibble of cinnamon cake herself.

Toby raised an eyebrow. "What kind of cake I am?"

"Your perfect cake," she said by way of explanation. "Usually I can tell as soon as I meet someone. Like, Amy's mom there is a pineapple upside-down cake, and her dad is a sour cream coffee cake with a crumbly blueberry center." (Here Amy's father raised his polka-dot cup of milk in the air and cheered, as though to confirm that this was indeed his perfect cake.) "But with you"—Cady closed her eyes—"for some reason it's a little harder."

Toby shifted in his seat. "Well, I . . ."

Cady popped her eyes open. "I guess I'll just have to think on it some more," she said. And the way her face lit up, she looked a bit like a baby bird who'd just discovered there was sunlight in the world.

Toby took another, bigger bite of cake, and began to settle into himself. Somehow, in this place, he felt happier, calmer, than he had in quite some time. As though perhaps the pebble in his shoe had managed to work its own way out.

It was a very nice sort of feeling.

He was finishing up his last bite of cake when Miss Mallory leaned over and whispered in his ear. "Just let me know when you're ready to fill out the paperwork," she told him. "I'll be so sorry to let her go, but . . ." Her gaze drifted across the table to Cady, giggling with Amy as they slapped playing cards down on the polka-dot cloth, and she set her hand over her heart again. "I can't say I didn't feel you coming."

Toby swallowed. "Sorry?" he said.

Miss Mallory turned her focus back to him. "That is why you came, isn't it?" she asked. "To adopt Cady?"

Toby felt the oddest sensation then, as though every emotion he'd ever had—happiness, sadness, worry, surprise—was colliding inside his body, battling to see which one of them might win. It was not so different from the sensation he'd felt once long ago, in that tiny village in Africa, when he'd been a very different man. For just one second, Toby was sure that his face had betrayed him, but he managed to shift everything back in place just in time.

"You do want to adopt her, don't you?" Miss Mallory asked, studying him carefully.

Across the table, Cady laughed again, slapping down another card. And in that moment, Toby knew. He'd give anything to be a father again.

"I'd love to adopt Cady," he said.

And that—*that*—was not at all a lie.

One Week Later . . .

V's Mystery Fudge Cake

—— *a cake that contains a delicious secret at its center* ——

FOR THE CAKE:

   1 ⅓ cups semisweet chocolate chips

   ⅓ cup flour

   ¼ tsp salt

   2 tsp unsweetened cocoa powder

   4 tbsp butter (½ stick), at room temperature
     (plus extra for greasing the muffin tins)

   ⅓ cup granulated sugar
     (plus extra for preparing the muffin tins)

   3 large eggs, at room temperature

FOR THE TOPPING:

   powdered sugar (optional)

1. Preheat oven to 400°F. Grease the bottoms and sides of six cups of a standard muffin tin with butter. Sprinkle the inside of the six buttered tins with granulated sugar, and tap to distribute it evenly.

2. In a double boiler or a heatproof bowl fitted into a saucepan of simmering water, carefully melt the chocolate chips over low heat, stirring often. Remove from heat and allow to cool, about 10 to 15 minutes.

3. In a small bowl, whisk together the flour, salt, and cocoa powder. Set aside.

4. In a large bowl, cream the butter and granulated sugar with an electric mixer, on medium speed, until light and fluffy, about 1 to 2 minutes. Add the eggs, one at a time, beating well after each addition.

5. With a spoon or spatula, gradually stir the flour mixture into the batter until just combined. Do not overmix. Stir in the cooled melted chocolate and combine, again being careful not to overmix.

6. Pour the batter into the prepared muffin tins. Bake for 12 to 14 minutes, or until the tops of the cakes no longer jiggle when shaken lightly. Let the cakes stand 10 minutes in the tin before turning out onto serving plates. Dust with powdered sugar if desired. Recipe makes 6 mini mystery fudge cakes with deliciously gooey middles. Best served warm.

Cady

CADY HAD ONLY EVER DREAMED THAT THIS DAY WOULD COME—
the seventh and final day of her trial period with a new family.
But here she was, one week in with Toby. And everything was
going swimmingly. Well, maybe not *swimmingly*, but . . . fine.
Far from grand, but not horrible, either.

Truth be told, Toby didn't talk much. Reserved, Miss Mallory
would have called him—like a table at a fancy restaurant where
only a select few could sit and chat. And that made it difficult to
get to know him, to figure out what might make their new little
family go from *fine* to *magnificent*. But Cady had a secret
weapon. That very morning, while Toby was off on his airport
run, Cady had baked him a yellow cake with chocolate frosting.

She wasn't entirely sure if it was Toby's *perfect* cake, but it was worth a try. She could smell it now, sweet and luscious and minutes from ready, as she searched for wildflowers between the Emporium's cracked porch slats.

The good news was that Miss Mallory had not yet come to retrieve Cady from her new home, as she'd done with all of Cady's previous trial families. And if Cady could hang on just a few hours more, then that very night, at the Fifty-Third Sunshine Bakers of America Annual Cake Bakeoff, Miss Mallory would officially declare whether or not Cady and Toby were a perfect match for each other. Whether Cady could finally have her own Adoption Day party and bake her own cake.

It was a big day indeed, and not just because it was the first time Cady had ever managed to use both of her guest tickets for the bakeoff. Cady tried to soothe the ache she felt in her chest, dull and worrying, whenever she thought too hard about leaving Miss Mallory and the orphanage for good. A worrying ache seemed a small price to pay for a perfect family.

As Cady plucked a yellow dandelion from a mess of weeds outside the Emporium's front door, Mrs. Asher's dusty red hatchback pulled to a stop in the driveway (the only car there beside the Owner's). Cady raced to greet her.

"Hello, there, sweetie," Mrs. Asher said, tucking the red whatever-it-was that she'd been knitting under one arm. She gave Cady a quick hug and hurried to the other side of the car to open the passenger's door. "Cady, this is V." Cady took a long look at the woman sitting in the passenger's seat, staring through the windshield at the Emporium. She was a mystery fudge cake, Cady was sure of it—a circular chocolate cake with a gooey chocolate center hidden inside it. "She doesn't talk. Take this bag, will you? Thanks."

"Do you need help getting her settled?" Cady asked, taking the bag of groceries Mrs. Asher handed her.

"I think we'll be okay," Mrs. Asher said. "You wouldn't happen to know where my children are, would you?"

"Marigold's practicing oboe"—Cady flicked an elbow toward an upstairs window, from which faint, stilted notes of music had been puttering for the last several minutes—"but I don't know about Zane and Will."

"Well, at least I can count on *one* of my children to do what she's supposed to." Mrs. Asher tugged a duffel bag out of the backseat. "You haven't seen my hairpin, by any chance?"

"Your hairpin?" Cady asked, finally realizing what it was about Mrs. Asher that seemed so different this morning. With her brown curls strewn wildly about her face, instead of tightly up in a bun the way they'd been all week, Mrs. Asher somehow looked a decade older. (Although perhaps, Cady thought, that had more to do with the whole moving-to-a-lost-luggage-store-with-three-children-while-her-husband-found-a-summer-job-in-New-Jersey-to-pay-for-the-repairs-to-their-apartment-from-a-rogue-hot-air-balloon-attack situation.) "I haven't seen it," Cady told her. "Sorry."

"I've never misplaced the thing. Not once in eleven years. But I guess with all the commotion this week I must've . . ." She sniffed the air. "Are you baking a cake?" Cady nodded. "It smells delicious. Marigold loved the one you made her, you know."

Cady smiled. She'd baked Marigold a lime pound cake the day the Ashers had moved in last week, and the girls had been fast friends ever since.

In the passenger's seat, V finally seemed to snap out of her trance. She held the duffel bag while Mrs. Asher helped her with her seat belt.

"What kind of cake are you making today?" Mrs. Asher asked.

Cady shifted the groceries to her hip and twirled the small bunch of yellow wildflowers in her left hand, watching the petals spin in dizzy circles. They were nothing like the dazzling purple petunias and multicolored pansies Miss Mallory cared for at the Home for Lost Girls, but they made Cady ache just the slightest for the place all the same. She looked up at Mrs. Asher. "Did you know you're a honey cake?" she said. "Rich with dark sweetness, and a surprising kick of spices."

Mrs. Asher helped V to her feet. "That is just *remarkable*," she said, shaking her head. "You're right, that does sound like exactly the perfect cake."

Cady looked down at her feet. "I'll have to make it for you sometime."

She felt the warm hand on her shoulder before she saw it. "Sweetheart?" Mrs. Asher said. "Everything okay?"

Cady bit her bottom lip. "I just want Toby to be happy with me, is all." What if the *reason* he was so reserved was that Cady wasn't the daughter he'd always dreamed of? What if, tonight at the bakeoff, he told Miss Mallory to go ahead and take Cady back?

Mrs. Asher opened her mouth to reply, but just at that moment, the wordless woman—V—made a noise like a startled horse. She dropped her duffel bag, right in the dirt, and when Cady looked up, she saw that the woman was staring at her.

V bolted for the Emporium door.

"Oh dear," Mrs. Asher said, rescuing the duffel. Her gaze followed V to the door. *Wha-pop!* went the wood against the frame. "She's had a difficult week," she told Cady.

Cady nodded.

"Before I forget . . ." Mrs. Asher hoisted the duffel to her shoulder and drew the red whatever-it-might-be from underneath her arm. With quick fingers she worked the needles through the yarn, finishing off the last row of loops, then snipped the loose end with a pair of scissors she pulled from who knew where. She traded the object to Cady for the bag of groceries. "This is for you."

It was a knitted red apron, perfect for cake-baking. Cady ran her fingers over the knotty red flowers stitched into it. It was the first piece of clothing that anyone had ever made her. "Thank you," she said.

Mrs. Asher squeezed her hand. "Of course. And Cady?" Cady

looked up from the apron. "All a parent really wants from his child is her happiness. So if you're happy, Toby will be, too."

Cady was bending down to pick a particularly beautiful wild-flower when she saw the plume of dirt curling down Argyle Road. At the far end of the drive, Cady could just make out a man on a bicycle, kicking up more and more dust as he headed ever closer. The man was huge, towering, even on a bicycle (although he rode it well). He was wearing a gray suit. And no matter how hard Cady squinted, she couldn't determine the man's age. He might have been forty, he might have been older.

There was a single powder blue suitcase strapped to the back of his bicycle.

The man rode right up to the front door. He swung a leg easily over the center bar of his bike and leaned the contraption against a dying hedge. "Good morning," he greeted Cady, unhooking the suitcase from the back.

"Morning," Cady replied.

The man bent down and picked up the flowers Cady hadn't realized she'd dropped. He handed them to her, a sideways sort of grin on his face. It was a grin that suggested he knew more about the world than he was letting on.

From the bottom of his suit jacket, she could make out several bits of knotted rope.

"Thanks," Cady said, taking the flowers.

"It's a funny thing, Fate."

Cady looked up from her flowers.

"There's no controlling what Fate hands you," the man went on, pulling the suitcase to his side. It was a very old suitcase, boxy and large as a small child, with worn corners and three small dimples near the left clasp. "And in my experience, it rarely seems to give you exactly what you need at the exact moment that you need it."

Cady wrinkled her eyebrows. "Sir?" she said. Maybe he thought she was someone else.

"Just remember this," he said. "It's the way we deal with what Fate hands us that defines who we are."

"Uh, sure," Cady said, turning her attention back to her wild-flowers. Maybe she'd find some more blossoms in the backyard. "I'll keep that in mi—"

But when she looked up again, the man in the gray suit was no longer there.

V

IT HAPPENED, NOW AND AGAIN, THAT V THOUGHT SHE SAW HER. Caroline. It was a common phenomenon, she'd been told, among parents who had lost their children. A photo in a magazine might remind her of Caroline's high school graduation, the way she'd mugged for the camera like she just *knew* this was the beginning of a fabulous adventure. A woman she passed in the grocery store might make V recall the last night she ever saw her—the way Caroline's secret smile should have hinted that she was about to run off to elope with a man her mother had never met (a "real charmer," that's about as much as Caroline would ever divulge about him). But no matter how many times it happened, the sting never lessened. When V had set eyes on the crow-haired girl with the flowers . . . it was too much.

Wha-pop! The door slammed shut against its frame as V stepped inside what she had surmised would be her new home. She took a slow look around. Racks of clothes, shelves of books, shoes, tennis rackets. This certainly wasn't a peanut butter factory anymore.

V had recognized the property immediately, as soon as it had appeared through the trees at the end of the long dirt road. The large white two-story building with the turrets on either side was a little worse for wear, maybe, but it was, without a doubt, the very same building from the old pictures on the jars. The Darlington Peanut Butter Factory. The roof of V's mouth watered even now with the memories.

There had never been anything like a jar of Darlington peanut butter. As soon as a dollop hit your tongue, your entire body melted into happiness. As a young girl, V hadn't been able to get enough of the stuff. Her parents hadn't, either. The whole town was nuts for it. The whole state. The factory could hardly churn out jars quickly enough, people bought so many. But the most amazing part of the whole operation—V remembered the stories distinctly—was that the factory's owner, the maker of every jar of peanut butter the place produced, had been Fair. She had not even a wisp of Talent, that's what they said, and yet somehow she had managed to stumble upon the world's most perfect peanut butter recipe. Thousands had tried to replicate it, but no one ever could. The Darlingtons kept the secret carefully guarded.

And then, suddenly, when V had been just a little girl, the factory had shut down. There was outrage throughout the town. Schoolchildren went on hunger strikes, refusing to eat their lunches. But it didn't make any difference.

There was no more peanut butter.

Rumor had it that the peanut butter maker's husband—a stodgy, surly type—shut down the factory after his wife's death, purely out of spite. Others swore that the woman's good-for-nothing son had gambled away the family's entire fortune.

V sighed, touching two fingers to her locket. Whatever the reason the factory had shut down all those years ago, it was a shame. She could very much use a taste of happiness at the moment.

The smell of vanilla and butter (a cake, perhaps?) guided V past the front door, and a soft melody, broken and stilted but beautiful all the same (an oboe?), led her farther into the room. There was a man not much older than she was, with salt-and-pepper hair, floating behind the large circular countertop in the center of the room. V might have supposed he was the owner of the establishment, except that he didn't seem to care at all about her presence. He was picking at his teeth with an enormous toothpick, and his nose was deep in a book V was quite familiar with. She recognized it by the color and contours of the words traipsing down the spine. But the words themselves? They might as well have been Spanish. Greek. Smashed ants on the page.

V sighed and drifted aimlessly up the stairs.

The Owner

THE ENORMOUS TOOTHPICK THE OWNER HAD FOUND THAT morning turned out to be perfect for dislodging that stubborn bit of sausage in his back molar, even if it did look a peculiar thing—beige and cracked and knobby, as wide as a rib of celery and as long as a pencil. He continued to chivy the sausage, his face deep in his book, as the front door let out a loud *wha-pop!* It wasn't long before it *wha-pop!*ed again, and then— *wha-pop!*—a third time. The Owner tapped his foot more quickly against the air. He'd *told* Toby all these new tenants would be nothing but a nuisance.

"Hello?" called a man's voice from the door. "Anyone here?"

The Owner flicked his eyes from his novel only long enough

to notice that the voice did not belong to a tenant, but (perhaps even more dreadfully) a customer. "Store's open," the Owner replied, still picking at his teeth. "Skis and prescription eyewear half off today."

The store had been sold out of skis and prescription eyewear for three years.

"Oh, I'm not looking to purchase anything," the man replied. His steps drew closer to the counter. "Actually, I was hoping I might sell *you* something."

The Owner hitched up his head. There, standing ten feet from the register, was a large man—towering, really—in a gray suit. He might have been forty, he might have been older.

He was carrying a powder blue suitcase.

The toothpick froze in the Owner's mouth. "Where did you find that?"

The man in the gray suit followed the Owner's gaze to the suitcase in his hand. It was sturdy but well-loved, boxy and large as a small child. "The St. Anthony's?" he asked. "It found me, actually, about eight years ago. Been around the world a couple times before we met, I believe." He chortled, while the Owner tapped a silent *rat-a-tat-tat* against the air.

Thirty-six. This was number thirty-six.

When Toby had returned from his luggage run last week, with the thirty-fifth St. Anthony's suitcase sitting on that malnourished orphan girl's lap, the Owner had thought *that* was a miracle (even if what he'd been searching for hadn't been inside). But now the thirty-sixth suitcase had just walked right up and found him, after all this time. It had taken the Owner over half a century, but at last every St. Anthony's suitcase ever made was inside the walls of his store.

"How much are you asking for it?" the Owner demanded.

"Oh, the suitcase isn't for sale. I'm in the business of utensils."

"Utensils?"

"And knickknacks, yes." The man in the gray suit grinned a sideways sort of grin. It was a grin that suggested he knew more about the world than he was letting on. "Small kitchen objects of all sorts, really."

The Owner noticed something peeking out from the bottom hem of the man's gray jacket. Several, were they . . . knots? Yes, knots of rope.

A gear clicked to life in the Owner's old rusty brain. He slipped the large toothpick into the pocket of his slacks (it let out a soft *clunk!* as it hit the jar beside it, but the man in the gray suit did not seem to notice). Then he lifted up the hinged section of the countertop and floated closer to the curious man. Slowly. Purposefully. He inspected him bottom to tip-tip-top.

"Have we met before?" the Owner asked.

The man in the gray suit laughed a guffaw of a laugh. "I think I'd remember a fellow like you," he said, pointing down at the

Owner's feet, two inches off the ground. "It's not every day you come across someone with such a Talent."

The Owner scratched his cheek. The click in his brain dulled to a low buzzing.

"So," the salesman continued, "might I interest you in any knickknacks, then? I've got mashers, peelers, dicers, whatever you like. You're my last stop before I head to the shop to pick up my hot air balloon." He drummed his large fingers on the suitcase, just beside the three small dimples. "I had quite an accident last week, lucky to be alive, really. But the thing's almost fixed. Which utensil did you say you were interested in?"

The Owner's old rusty brain shook itself back into action. He leaned across the countertop to clang open the register. "I'll take the whole lot," he told the salesman, "provided you sell me that suitcase as well." And, with an agility he hadn't been able to muster in years, the Owner swept his hands through the register drawers, plucking out every last bill. "That ought to be enough, don't you think?" He handed the salesman the money—all of it—without even bothering to count.

The man in the gray suit kept the sideways grin on his face as he handed over the suitcase. "Pleasure doing business with you," he said.

The Owner allowed himself a tiny breath of contentment as he took hold of the suitcase. Number thirty-six. "The pleasure was all mine," he said. And then he reached his right hand into his pants pocket for the jar, squeezing the icy chill out of his palm.

Plunk!

His feet firmly on the ground, the Owner stretched out his hand to shake.

Marigold

PLAYING THE OBOE ALWAYS MADE MARIGOLD'S MOUTH DRY AS cotton. She licked her lips and darted her eyes to the clock on the dresser.

Nine more minutes before her hour of practice was over. She sighed and began the song again. But no matter how hard she tried to position her tongue and her lips and her fingers the way Maestro Messina instructed, the notes still came out sour. She shot an anxious look at the freckled patch of skin on her wrist, where her red Talent bracelet with the shiny silver beads usually sat. Last night she'd slipped the bracelet over her bedpost before she went to sleep, the way she did every evening, but when she'd woken up this morning it had vanished. She couldn't find it anywhere. Marigold felt almost naked without it.

A soft creak in the floorboards compelled Marigold to look up from her music book.

Standing there, seeming lost and a little bewildered, was a woman of about sixty. She was thin, wiry, with short gray hair. Marigold could just make out the locket around her neck, the silver oval with the single letter engraved on it.

"You must be V," Marigold said, even though she knew the woman wouldn't reply. It was only polite, in any case. She set the oboe in her lap. "I'm Marigold."

The woman continued to stare at her.

No, she wasn't staring at *Marigold*. She was staring at the oboe.

"You want to see it?" Marigold asked, inviting the woman into the room with a wave of her arm.

Seeming to understand the offer, V picked her way over to the bed and sat down gingerly. Marigold handed her the oboe, wondering if perhaps this mysterious woman was a Talented oboist. Wouldn't that be something? If Marigold discovered her Talent in less than a minute?

The woman held the oboe like it was a popsicle about to melt through her fingers.

"Like this," Marigold said, motioning with her hands. "And your lips go . . ." She rolled her top lip, just the way Maestro

Messina had showed her so many times. "Yes! Just like that. Then your fingers go on the keys like"—she helped V place them—"and you blow."

V had never played an oboe before, that was clear from her first weak note. And she certainly wasn't Talented, that was clear from the second one. But she had . . . something. Something that Marigold couldn't put her finger on.

"You're starting out better than I did," Marigold told her with a smile. "Here, breathe from down here." She placed a hand on her own stomach, right in the gut. "That's where your power comes from." And although Marigold knew that V couldn't understand the words she was saying, somehow she deciphered the meaning. V began to sit up a little straighter, breathe a little deeper. "Wonderful!" Marigold cried when the next note came out clearer.

"I see you've met our newest housemate." Marigold looked up to see her mother in the door frame. "Is she bothering you while you practice?"

Marigold shook her head. "Nah," she said, turning her attention back to V, who was experimenting with her fingers on different keys. "She's not bad, actually."

Mrs. Asher glanced at her watch. "Goodness, it's later than I thought. I have to get to the yarn shop. Can you do me a favor, Mari?"

"Yeah?"

"I meant to put together a care package for your father this morning, but I've run clear out of time. Will you pack it up for me? Everything's in a pile on my bed, but it needs a box. Or maybe the Owner will let you use one of those old suitcases downstairs, if you ask nicely."

Marigold's lips turned into a pout. "Aw, Mom, can't Zane do it? Cady said she'd help me Talent-hunt before the bakeoff."

Her mother's cheeks went taut. "Zane is watching Will at the moment, so, no, young lady, he can't do it."

Marigold had no idea what her brother was up to at that moment, but it certainly wasn't watching Will. Up to no good, more likely. Just like always. Marigold knew, from the letter she'd shamefully steamed open before secretly resealing and returning it to her mother's car, that Zane was in it up to his neck this time. Talking back, ditching class, spitting (of course). Apparently he had even been accused of stealing valuables from his classmates and teachers to sell at Louie's Pawn Shop in town.

"You're my responsible one, Marigold," her mother went on, "and I would like you to do this simple favor for your father. You'll have plenty of time for Talent-fishing later."

"Talent-*hunting*," Marigold grumbled, but she knew her arguing was over.

Maybe it wouldn't hurt if she were a *little* more like Zane, a pain in the neck who didn't care what anybody thought of him. She'd spit at the world—*ptew!*—and see how they liked it.

"Thank you, sweetie." Mrs. Asher's voice softened when she realized she'd won. "I already filled out a label for the package with your father's New Jersey address. Make sure to get it together before the mail pickup today, will you? Toby said the postwoman usually comes about noon."

"Okay," Marigold replied. *Someone* had to be the good one, after all.

Will

ON HIS HANDS AND KNEES, WILL CRAWLED AROUND ANOTHER corner. "Sally?" he called again. The name echoed through the twists and turns of the air vent. *"Sally-Sally-Sally?"* Will perked his ears up as the sound faded, but he did not hear his ferret's telltale *click-click-clack.*

Sally had been lost all morning. She'd probably found something shiny and gone off to hide it. Will climbed as the vent sloped up, up, up to the second floor of the Emporium. He clung tight to the walls with his fingertips.

"Sally-Sally-Sally?"

Nothing but dust.

Will continued to search until he found a trickle of light,

shining up into the vent. "Sally?" he whispered. There was a noise, like a door being tucked closed. Belly flat, Will scooched his way to the zigzag of light and pressed his face against the cold metal grate, peering down onto the bedroom below.

It wasn't Sally.

Will couldn't make out the face of the man banging objects about on the bookshelf, but he knew right away that it was the Owner because of his salt-and-pepper hair. It was the Owner, no question.

So why were the man's feet planted firmly on the ground?

The Owner

THE OWNER THOUGHT, AS HE SEARCHED THROUGH HIS bookshelf, that perhaps he heard a soft scuttling noise from the ceiling above, but when he looked up, he saw nothing. Just his old ears playing tricks on him again. He glanced at the St. Anthony's suitcase waiting patiently on his tattered bedspread. The Owner was desperate to open it, to look inside. But it had been fifty-three years already—he could certainly savor this moment the way it was meant to be savored.

The bookshelf along the far wall of the Owner's bedroom was lined with jars, top to bottom. To someone who didn't know any better, they would probably look like simple peanut butter jars. All of them unmarked. All of them empty. But the Owner could tell them apart, and they most certainly were not empty.

This was his collection of Talents. Talents for origami and dog-training and computer-repair and whistling, and dozens of others he'd managed to nab over the years. The Owner had always believed that there was really only one Talent you needed in this world: The Talent for appropriating other people's Talents.

Selecting a jar from the back, one which had not yet been filled, the Owner—*switt-tsk-schwap!*—unscrewed the lid. Then he lifted his right hand above the empty jar and squeezed it into a fist. Tighter and tighter he squeezed, until at last . . .

Plunk!

Where just a moment ago there had been nothing, now suddenly there was the Talent the Owner had plucked from the man in the gray suit, clean and condensed and opaque, like an ice cube. The Owner had seen the sight a thousand times, but he never tired of it.

As the Owner reached for the lid to the jar, the Talent began to dissipate, just as the Talents always did if you left them to their own devices. A fine mist rose out of the jar, higher, higher, straight into the air vent above. The Owner thought he heard a soft sniffle escape from the vent, but when he shot his eyes up to check, there was nothing. Tricks from his old ears again.

He returned his attention to his Talents.

Will

WILL PRESSED HIS FACE HARDER AGAINST THE GRATE, UNTIL HE was sure the metal zigzags were patterning his nose. When he unintentionally sniffed up some of the mist, he had the strangest desire to tie a knot.

Down below, the Owner screwed the lid down tight on the jar in his hand. And, as Will watched, the ice cube that had appeared from nothing only moments before evaporated to mist inside the jar, and then thinned into a haze, and then disappeared completely. Within the span of an instant, the jar appeared just as empty as before. The Owner set it back on the shelf with the others, then pulled a new jar from his pocket. He opened it, raised his hand above it, fingers stretched taut, and again a mysterious icy stone appeared, just below the old man's skin. But this time, the ice cube melted into the Owner's palm, and his feet began to rise—one inch, then two—until he was floating above the ground, the way Will was accustomed to seeing him.

Will tensed his muscles the way the knights in his storybooks would if they'd just caught an evil wizard doing something suspicious. He'd been searching for Sally, but he just might have found an adventure.

Down below, the Owner crossed to the bed with the suitcase on it. He was up to no good, Will was certain of it.

And then the Owner took something new from his pocket, and began to pick his teeth with it.

Beige.

Cracked.

Knobby.

As wide as a rib of celery and as long as a pencil.

The Owner was picking his teeth with Will's mother's hairpin.

Suddenly, Will wasn't Will anymore. Suddenly he was *Sir* Will, a brave knight whose job it was to retrieve precious stolen objects from spooky evil wizards.

With the quick thinking and courage of the very best knights from the very best storybooks, Sir Will wrenched the grate off the bottom of the vent. (It was heavier than it looked, but not too heavy for a knight.)

Sir Will leapt to the floor. (It was a long leap, and scary, but not too scary for a knight.)

And before the evil wizard could roar out a "Just what do you think you're—" Sir Will had kicked him square in the shin and snatched his mother's prized possession from his old, grizzled fingers.

Then Sir Will ran.

Toby's (Not Quite Perfect) Yellow Cake With Chocolate Frosting

certainly the perfect cake for somebody

FOR THE CAKE:

   2 ½ cups flour (plus extra for preparing the cake pan)

   1 ½ tsp baking powder

   ¼ tsp baking soda

   ½ tsp salt

   1 cup butter (2 sticks), at room temperature
   (plus extra for greasing the cake pan)

   1 ½ cups granulated sugar

   2 tsp vanilla

   3 large eggs, at room temperature

   1 cup milk, at room temperature

FOR THE FROSTING:

   ⅔ cup semisweet chocolate chips

   ¾ cup butter (1 ½ sticks), at room temperature

   3 ½ cups powdered sugar

   ½ cup milk, at room temperature

   1 tbsp vanilla

1. Preheat oven to 350°F. Lightly grease the bottoms of two
8-inch round cake pans with butter. Using the cake pans as a

template, trace two circles onto wax paper and cut them out, placing one wax circle in the bottom of each pan. Grease both pans with butter again, covering the wax paper as well as the sides of the pan. Sprinkle the inside of the pans lightly with flour, and tap the pans to distribute it evenly.

2. In a medium bowl, whisk together the flour, baking powder, baking soda, and salt. Set aside.

3. In a large bowl, beat the butter and granulated sugar with an electric mixer on medium-high speed until fluffy, about 2 to 3 minutes. Add the vanilla, then the eggs, one at a time, beating until well combined.

4. Reducing the speed on the mixer to low, add about a third of the flour mixture to the batter, combining well. Add about half of the milk and combine. Then add another third of the flour mixture, the last of the milk, and then the last of the flour, combining well each time.

5. Pour the batter into the pans and smooth the tops. Bake for 25 to 30 minutes, or until a toothpick comes out clean. Cool completely before frosting.

6. While the cake is cooling, make the frosting: In a double boiler or a heatproof bowl fitted into a saucepan of simmering water, carefully melt the chocolate chips. Remove from the heat and allow to cool.

7. In a large bowl, cream the butter with a mixer on medium speed until fluffy, about 3 minutes. Gradually add about half of the powdered sugar, blending well. Beat in 2 tbsp of the milk and all of the vanilla, then beat in the remaining powdered sugar, followed by the remaining milk. Add the cooled melted chocolate to the butter mixture and beat until smooth.

8. When the cakes are completely cooled, place one cake layer on a plate and spread a thin layer of frosting on top. Repeat with the second cake layer, and cover the whole cake with frosting.

Toby

TOBY WRESTLED A SLIM GREEN SUITCASE OUT OF THE BED OF his truck. It had been a small load from the airport this morning, and not a single St. Anthony's suitcase. The old man would be disappointed.

The front door of the Emporium slammed shut with a *wha-pop!* and out came an enormous man in a gray suit. "Can you tell me where I might catch the bus to River Street?" the man asked Toby as he walked by.

Toby set the suitcase down in the dirt. "You'll want the number 6," he replied. "There's a stop just up the road. To your left at the end of Argyle."

"Thank you kindly."

"Excuse me!" Toby called as the man in the gray suit started down the path. "Aren't you forgetting your bike?" He pointed to the dinged-up bicycle propped against a brown hedge.

"Never seen it before," the man replied with a sideways sort of grin. It was a grin that suggested that he knew more about the world than he was letting on.

He walked off down the road.

Toby shook his head and began hauling his load of suitcases inside. The store was quiet, except for the soft strains of stilted oboe music. The old man was not at his post behind the counter.

It was on his last run from the truck that Toby noticed her. He'd assumed that the person playing the oboe was the curly-haired girl, Marigold. But when he happened to glance at Marigold's bedroom window, it wasn't her head of hair he saw, but a close-cropped gray cut instead—and just enough of her face to recognize her.

Suddenly Toby felt unsettled in a way he hadn't all week. His skin prickled, his cheeks grew hot. He banged closed the back of his truck and lugged the last two suitcases—*wha-pop!*— inside the Emporium to the small office behind the kitchen. He had to leave. They *both* had to leave. This wretched place had been pushing Toby away for years, but now that there was someone else to think about, Toby found himself actually listening. The Lost Luggage Emporium was no place for a child, he knew that for a fact. Not with the old man and his single-minded whims.

But how to explain that to Cady, without having to explain too much?

Toby had mostly ironed out the last of his nerves when a slender shadow appeared across the top of the bag he was unzipping. He jerked up his head with a start, but it was only Cady.

"Oh," he said, stretching a smile across his face. "Hello there."

She blinked at him for a moment, as though adjusting her eyes to the light. "What are you doing?" she asked at last.

Toby pulled up a stool for her next to him. "Just sorting through my haul from the airport," he told her. "Which things to sell, which things to toss." He plucked a well-read copy of *Face Value* out of the bag in front of him and pitched it into the Toss pile.

"I made you some cake," Cady said, holding out the small plate with the fork balanced just so. "These are for you, too." A glass of yellow wildflowers. She set them on the small desk littered with papers.

"Oh, Cady, you didn't have to do that."

"Try the cake," she insisted.

Toby took a bite. Yellow cake with a creamy chocolate frosting. He pressed the moist crumbs to the roof of his mouth and closed his eyes, wishing that he might someday be the man who was the perfect fit for such a cake.

"I'm still working on it," Cady said, leaning forward on the edge of her stool, watching him chew.

"Well, it's wonderful." He took another bite.

Cady tilted her head to the side. "You don't talk much, you know," she said suddenly.

Toby laughed, coughing on a few crumbs. He was growing to quite like this wide-eyed little girl. "I suppose I can be standoffish sometimes," he admitted. "What would you like to know?"

Cady shrugged. "I just want to know about *you*," she said. "To . . . to help me figure it out, about the cake."

Toby thought about that. "Let's see," he said slowly. "What can I tell you that might be interesting?" Toby scraped the edge of his fork along the plate, collecting some stray frosting. He didn't want to lie, not more than he had already, but what could he tell her? He searched his brain until he found a memory, a good and true one, that she might enjoy. "When I was younger I used to travel," he said at last.

Cady sat up a little straighter, interested. "What sorts of places did you go to?"

"Oh"—he slipped another bite of cake onto his tongue—"everywhere," he said, chewing. "Europe, Asia, Australia. If I got an itch, I hopped on a plane and flew clear across the world to scratch it." Cady laughed. "Once we even—I went to Africa to . . ."

To get married. They'd flown to Africa to get married, and

they'd stayed for the adventure. And what an adventure it had been! More than they had bargained for, that was for sure. As soon as their delightful baby daughter was born, they knew it was going to be the adventure of a lifetime. It had all been so wonderful.

Until, suddenly, it was anything but.

"I went to Africa once," Toby finished at last.

Beside him, Cady let out a breath, leaning back against a tall stack of suitcases. "I'd love to go somewhere someday," she said.

Toby scooped the last bite of cake onto his fork. "How about today?" Here was his chance. They'd call it a bit of travel, and she'd never have to know the real reason for escaping this dreadful place. "We can go anywhere you want. Europe, Ecuador, Ethiopia." He tensed his fingers excitedly around the cake plate. His skin felt warm, tingly, at the very idea. "We could be on a plane in an hour if we hurry. Start a new life anywhere at all. What about Switzerland? Wouldn't that be nice, just you and me and some goats?" Cady fingered the knotted red flowers on her apron. "Or maybe something more metropolitan?" Toby suggested. "Wouldn't you just *love* to live in Paris? You could see the Eiffel Tower from your bedroom window, what do you think of that? You must be sick of living in this old place already. The grumpy old man alone is enough to make someone want to leave forever."

Cady bent to pick up the fork that had fallen off Toby's cake plate.

"Cady?"

She looked up. "Well . . ." she said slowly, "we can't go tonight, can we? Because of the bakeoff."

Toby shifted his face into a smile. "Of course," he said. "Tomorrow, then. I mean, assuming it all goes well with Miss Mallory."

"Do you think . . . ?" Cady's voice grew so quiet, it was almost a whisper. "I do want to stay, you know," she said. "I really like it here. At the Emporium, I mean."

Toby let her take his empty cake plate. There were too many things, too many people, who could so easily ruin the life he and Cady had started together. But there was no easy way to tell her all of that. "I really should get back to my work," he said instead. "Thanks again for the cake."

"You liked it?"

He smiled again, a sincere one. The smiling *was* getting easier, this week. "I loved it," he told her.

Toby might have failed at being a father once, he thought as Cady headed back to the kitchen, but there was no way he was going to fail again. He'd do whatever it took, but he was not going to fail.

The Owner

THE KID WAS OUT THE DOOR WITH THE TOOTHPICK BEFORE the Owner had even realized what happened. The Owner's first instinct was to chase after him, but then his eyes fell to the powder blue suitcase on the bed. What did he care about a lousy toothpick when his whole life might be in that suitcase?

Number thirty-six.

The last suitcase of them all.

The Owner positioned himself directly in front of the suitcase, ran his fingers over the three dimples by the left clasp. This was the one, he was certain. He flipped open the first latch, then the second.

Utensils. Dozens and dozens of knickknacks and gadgets

were inside. Rolling pins. Eggbeaters. Thermometers. Scoopers, scrapers, slicers, slotted spoons. Toast tongs. Mashers, peelers, corers, mincers, pitters, graters, grinders. Whisks and bags and brushes.

The Owner flicked them onto the bed by the handful. They littered the bedspread and clattered to the floor. In one of the suitcase's inner pockets was a black ceramic bird, its yellow beak angled up and open. Useless.

With one smart jerk, the Owner ripped the faded flowered lining down the seam. He held his breath and felt inside.

Nothing.

He checked again.

Nothing.

Letting out a terrible roar, the Owner snatched the suitcase off the bed, stormed to the hallway, and chucked it down the stairs. It landed with a *thud* on top of the circular wooden counter.

Fifty-three years. He'd spent fifty-three years searching, tracking down every St. Anthony's suitcase ever made, and it wasn't there.

His mother's peanut butter recipe wasn't there.

Cady

CADY HAD JUST DROPPED TOBY'S CAKE PLATE IN THE SUDSY sink when she heard the *thud* from the main storeroom floor. She scuttled out of the kitchen and looked to the top of the stairs just in time to make out the Owner's surly face. He growled at her and then slammed shut his bedroom door.

Toby was right about him—he *was* a grumpy old man.

Flung carelessly atop the circular counter in the center of the room was the thing that Cady assumed must be the source of the Owner's rage (as well as the *thud*)—a single powder blue suitcase, with three small dimples near the left clasp. It looked exactly like the suitcase the curious man in the gray suit had unstrapped from his bicycle (and also quite a bit like the other powder blue suitcases Cady had noticed under the countertop—some sort of collection of the Owner's, she figured).

Cady stood on her toes at the counter and pried the suitcase open carefully, wondering what about a piece of old luggage could possibly have made the Owner so furious. But all she found, inside one of the pockets, was a small ceramic bird, its yellow beak wide open in a whistle.

Perhaps the Owner really hated birds.

As Cady moved to snap closed the top, something fluttered out of the ripped lining, just flittered to the floor, as though Fate had wanted her to find it. A slip of paper. Cady picked it off the ground. It was brown like a fallen leaf, and brittle with age. Its creases were raised like scars. As she slowly unfolded it, one corner crumbled completely to bits.

PERFECT PEANUT BUTTER

That's what was written across the top of the paper. Cady bit her bottom lip as she read the recipe. If anything could make a person less of a grump, she thought, it was a cake baked specifically for him. And maybe, if the Owner were just a little less grumpy, Toby might want to stick around a while longer.

He might want Cady to stick around, too.

Cady hadn't so much as finished the thought, however, when the words of the man in the gray suit scampered into her head.

It's the way we deal with what Fate hands us that defines who we are. Cady shook them free. With the recipe clasped gingerly in her fingertips, she shut the suitcase and slid it underneath the countertop with its brothers. Then she headed to the kitchen. There were only a few hours before the bakeoff, and she had a cake to make.

Zane

ZANE HEARD THE *THUD* ON THE COUNTERTOP OF THE MAIN
storeroom floor, but he ignored it. Tucked away in the electronics corner, Zane did his best to tread lightly, quietly. It was silly,
perhaps, to think he could keep ahead of the trouble he knew
was coming, but darned if he wasn't going to try anyway.
Because even if the letter from that old bat Principal Piles
seemed to have disappeared in the chaos of the move (his parents had yet to mention it, and in Zane's vast experience with
trouble, when parents read such letters, they usually mentioned
them right away), Zane's problems hadn't disappeared. Sooner
or later, one way or another, Zane's parents were going to hear
from the principal. They were going to have to decide whether

or not to send him to boarding school. And there was a chance—slim perhaps, but a chance nonetheless—that Zane could cut the trouble off at the pass.

Zane pulled a pair of expensive-looking headphones off a shelf and examined them carefully before tucking them inside his pocket. They would fetch a pretty fair price at Louie's Pawn Shop (well, as fair a price as Louie ever gave). And with enough trips to Louie's, Zane just might (perhaps, maybe) be able to cover some of the cost of the repairs for that stupid hole in his family's apartment wall. Nobody would send a thoughtful, supportive boy like that to boarding school. Well, it was worth a shot, anyway. As long as Zane's parents didn't figure out how *truly* . . .

WORTHLESS.

When Zane's pockets were stuffed almost to bursting, he searched the store for the perfect container to store his goods in. If he remembered correctly, under the circular counter there was a stash of seriously old blue suitcases. The Owner would never notice if one of those was missing.

On his hands and knees, Zane pulled out one of the suitcases. *St. Anthony's*, the scrawl of silver thread across the top announced. There were three small dimples by the left clasp. Zane opened it up. The lining was torn. He yanked out a second case from the collection to see if perhaps it was in slightly better shape. Positioning this second suitcase next to the other—just to the left—Zane opened the clasps. Torn as well, in exactly the same spot. Zane shrugged. He supposed it would have to do. Into the suitcase went the cameras, the leather wallets, the rings, the belt buckles. Anything that might score a few dollars.

Zane hadn't realized just how much he'd miss his old home before they moved into the Emporium. He'd never been the kind of kid who felt particularly homesick when his family went away on vacation or he spent a week at camp. *What was so great about a tiny, cramped apartment?* he'd always wondered. *With everybody smooshed together, poking into your business all the time?* Nothing. That's what he'd always thought.

But if they *did* send him to boarding school . . . Zane swiped at his nose. Maybe it wasn't so bad, having your business poked into just a little bit.

Zane was just emptying his last pocket into the suitcase when he heard a startling *skitter-skitter-CRASH!* And suddenly, in a flash of fur and claws, Will's pet ferret, Sally, *whomp*ed down from the overhead air vent, right into Zane's spiky hair.

"Aaaagh!" Zane batted at her wildly until she skittered down his neck, across his chest, and buried herself inside the suitcase of loot, where she promptly became entangled in the pricey headphones.

"Sally!" Zane shouted, digging into the suitcase to pull her out by her scruff. "Don't you dare break any of my stuff, you little weasel."

Sally spit out the shiny bit of whatever it was she'd been hoarding to let out a frantic *click-click-clack!* of protest.

"Get out of here!" Zane advised her, tossing her to the floor. "Why don't you go find Will?"

Sally narrowed her eyes threateningly at Zane, but she scurried off just the same. Zane shook his head. *Stay ahead of the trouble,* he reminded himself. *You need to stay ahead of the trouble.*

WORTHLESS.

Zane jumped up on his heels. All he needed now was some way to get to Louie's and sell his stuff. A bicycle, maybe. A bicycle would be perfect. Leaving his loot in the suitcase for just a moment, he wandered off to see if he might be able to find one.

Will

SIR WILL WAITED UNTIL HE WAS SURE THE COAST WAS CLEAR before popping out of the air vent onto the main storeroom floor. There was no way the evil wizard would ever find him. Sir Will was too good at hiding. He zipped across the room until he reached the circular countertop in the center. There he found a pair of powder blue suitcases. Perfect. Sir Will flipped open the top of one of them—the one on the right. It had three small dimples by the left clasp, and it was just large enough for a small child.

Checking that no one was watching, Sir Will crawled inside, curling himself into a tight little ball against the torn inner lining. (Sir Will had somehow lost one of his shoes along the way, but knights didn't care about things like that.) He pulled the lid securely over his body and clutched at his mother's precious hairpin, waiting for his heart to stop racing. He breathed in deep. His pulse slowed. His eyes drifted closed. And safe in the darkness of the warm blue suitcase, Sir Will drifted . . . off . . . to . . . *sleep.*

Marigold's Lime Pound Cake

—— a cake that contains more than a little zest and zing ——

FOR THE CAKE:

- 4 large eggs, at room temperature
- ½ tsp vanilla
- 2 tsp grated lime zest (from approximately 2 limes)
- 2 tbsp lime juice (from approximately 1 lime)
- 1 cup butter (2 sticks), at room temperature
  (plus extra for greasing the cake pan)
- 1 ¼ cups granulated sugar
- ½ tsp salt
- 2 cups flour

1. Preheat oven to 325°F. Grease a 9-by-5-inch loaf pan with butter.

2. In a small bowl, whisk together the eggs, vanilla, lime zest, and lime juice. Set aside.

3. In a large bowl, beat the butter with an electric mixer on medium-high speed, until fluffy, about 2 minutes. Add the sugar and the salt and beat, starting on low speed and then increasing to medium-high, until well combined, about 2 minutes more. Slowly add the egg mixture and beat until well combined, about 3 minutes.

4. Reducing the speed on the mixer to low, gradually add the flour to the batter, and beat until just combined.

5. Pour the batter into the pan and smooth the top. Bake for 60 to 70 minutes, or until a toothpick comes out clean. Cool completely before serving.

Marigold

MARIGOLD PICKED HER WAY DOWN THE STAIRS, HER ARMS piled so high with shirts and pants and things for her father that she practically tumbled to her death three times. A suitcase. She needed a suitcase to ship the care package.

At the foot of the circular counter in the center of the room, Marigold spied a pair of old powder blue suitcases. *Perfect*, she thought, making her way over. She set down her father's things and flipped open one of the cases—the one on the left.

It wasn't empty.

Inside the suitcase was an impressive stash of odds and ends. Watches and cameras and jewelry. A pair of fancy head-phones. Expensive-looking gadgets. Things that a delinquent spiky-haired kid just might steal and sell at a pawn shop. Marigold gritted her teeth. *When* was her brother going to learn that he couldn't just—

Something shiny caught Marigold's eye. Three silver beads, strung onto a short length of red thread, plopped carelessly on top of the rest of Zane's loot in the suitcase.

Her Talent bracelet.

"*Zane!*" Marigold hollered. She slapped the bracelet onto her wrist. That little fink had actually *stolen* her Talent bracelet, and he'd been planning to sell it. Didn't he care about anybody but himself?

Well, maybe he'd learn to care a little more if he didn't have his precious stolen treasure to sell. Her cheeks puffed with rage, Marigold flung her father's things on top of Zane's plunder and squeezed closed the lid of the suitcase. She secured the clasps tight. From her pocket she produced the label for her father's hotel in New Jersey. *Let's see what our parents have to say about Zane's new hobby,* she thought.

Wha-pop!

There was a noise from the doorway. Marigold jerked her head up, the address label still in her hand. It was a mailwoman, her satchel of letters hanging at her side. She noticed Marigold and headed her way.

"I'm Gloria," the mailwoman greeted her. Marigold stood to accept the small bundle of letters that Gloria handed over. "Any parcels or packages to go out today?"

Marigold nodded quickly. "Yep," she said. "A big one. Let me just . . ." She peeled off the back of the mailing label and bent to slap it on the suitcase—the one on the right. She secured the clasps tight.

"Here, let me help," Gloria said, reaching out to hoist the suitcase to her side. "Ooh, that's heavy. I'll charge the shipping to the Emporium's account, is that okay?" Marigold nodded, and Gloria headed to the door, her muscles straining with the weight of the suitcase.

Marigold smiled to herself, smoothing her bracelet over her wrist as Gloria *wha-pop!*ed open the front door and loaded the suitcase into the back of her truck.

And then Marigold noticed it, across the storeroom floor: a small boys' sneaker. Marigold crossed the room to snatch it up.

Will's left shoe.

An uncomfortable unease prickled Marigold's cheeks. Slowly, she returned to the circular counter, where there was now only one powder blue suitcase.

Its clasps were secured tight.

Slowly, Marigold knelt down.

Slowly, she opened the case.

There were the contents of her father's care package. Shirts and pants and underwear, the special shampoo he liked so much. Zane's loot was there, too. All just as she'd packed it. Marigold turned back to the shoe in her hand, just as the mail truck's tires began to scrape across the gravel parking lot.

"*Stop!*" Marigold hollered, leaping to her feet. She waved the shoe as she ran out the door, down the driveway, across the dirt road. "*STOP!*"

But it was too late. The mail truck was already gone. It kicked up dust as it rolled down Argyle Road, the powder blue suitcase hopping up and down in the back, as fitfully as Marigold's stomach inside her.

Marigold had the worst suspicion that she'd just mailed off her little brother to New Jersey.

Will

Rattle.

Rattle.

Thump-a-thump-a-thump-a.

Something was shaking, Will observed as he woke up. Something was shaking, and moving, and bumping. It was him: *He* was moving. *Rattle, rattle, thump-a-thump-a-thump-a.* And it was dark. Very dark. All Will could make out was a tiny sliver of light. He was curled up so tight, he could hardly move, and he was holding what he was pretty sure was his mother's hairpin. He was missing a shoe, too. His back ached from having been pressed so long against something solid, about the size and shape of a small ceramic bird.

Where *was* he?

Thump-a!

A suitcase, Will remembered. He was inside a suitcase. And now the suitcase was *moving*, probably on the back of a truck somewhere, heading who-knew-where.

Thump-a-thump-a-thump-a!

The truck swerved.

Screech!

The suitcase bounced up . . .

Fwoop!

. . . and then down . . .

Tha-WUNK!

. . . and then it rolled over, over, over down a hill . . .

Crash crash tumble crash!

. . . through a thicket of weeds and bushes . . .

Schwick-a-schwick-a-schwick-a!

. . . until it smashed . . .

Crack!

. . . into a small rock.

Ka-THUMP.

And Will toppled out, end over end over end.

Splat!

Will looked up at the blue sky and smiled.

He was *definitely* on an adventure now.

Miss Mallory

MISS MALLORY WAS SITTING AT THE PICNIC TABLE ON THE front lawn, reading a mystery. *Face Value*, by Victoria Valence. She'd been planning to work in her flower beds, the way she usually did to pass time between orphans, but she was currently facing a conundrum.

The man who owned the local nursery—the person who'd sold Miss Mallory all of her petunia bulbs and pansy seeds, fertilizer and planting tools and everything—had, just that morning, presented her with a gift. "I created them specially for you," he'd told her proudly. "My best customer."

Miss Mallory set her book in her lap to study the gift once more, staring back at her from atop the picnic table. It was a small carton of delicate purple flowers, unlike anything Miss Mallory had ever seen before. And yet at the same time, they were quite familiar. "A hybrid," the nursery owner had declared. "My own creation—an impeccable cross between a petunia and a pansy. Beautiful, aren't they?"

They certainly were. The flowers had the petunia's distinctive mauve hue and the pansy's particular petals. Even their scent was a perfect mix—combining the crisp freshness of a petunia with a pansy's delicate richness, creating a cool, clean aroma that was both invigorating and calming at once. Like a favorite aunt's perfume. No doubt about it: The new flowers would be a stunning addition to Miss Mallory's lawn.

The conundrum, however, was that Miss Mallory had no idea where to put them. Should she plant these new flowers in the petunia bed, to the left of the front door? Or would they be better suited with the pansies, to the right? Where did you put something that fit so perfectly in two very different places?

Miss Mallory turned back to her book. She should be spending this quiet time enjoying herself, she thought, since there were no orphans banging about. Less laundry to worry about. Fewer dishes to be washed. And yet here she was, fretting over flowers. She could only hope that, in the many quiet days that were sure to come, she'd learn to do a better job of relaxing. Because this was it, Miss Mallory knew. Cady had finally found her perfect family. The tug in Miss Mallory's chest had told her.

(It was trying to tell her something else, too, as it turned out, but Miss Mallory wasn't listening.)

"Aren't I in a sorry state?" she said to the flowers on the picnic table. "Take my last orphan away and I crumble to bits." She sighed. "Still, I do wish I had *something* to match."

The flowers, of course, had no response. But a hundred yards from the orphanage, in a thick patch of weeds and brush by the side of the windy highway, something else did.

Ka-THUMP.

Miss Mallory left her book on the picnic table to inspect the source of the noise. After several minutes she found it—a suitcase, busted open. It was old and worn and powder blue, as large as a small child, with three dimples near the left clasp and the words *St. Anthony's* stitched on the side in silver thread.

The suitcase was empty, save for a small black ceramic bird, nestled into an interior pocket. A hole was shaped in the creature's middle, purposefully, all the way from the bird's feet to its pointed yellow beak.

Miss Mallory tucked the bird into her pocket. She wasn't sure why, but somehow she was entirely certain that Fate had brought it to her.

Mrs. Asher

"**Mom, slow down! We're going to crash into a tree.**"

Dolores did not slow down. There was no slowing down when your youngest son was missing. Those idiots at the post office had said they had no idea what had happened to him, that the suitcase had just fallen off the truck somewhere. Which was not exactly the constructive sort of information she'd been looking for.

"Mom," Marigold said again. And even with her eyes glued to the road, Dolores could tell that Marigold was spinning that red bracelet of hers around her wrist in the way she did when she was upset. "At this speed we won't see him even if we pass him."

Dolores did her best to temper some of the fury that was

burning inside her. She pressed her right foot gently onto the brake to slow the car. "I just don't know what got into you," she told her daughter.

Marigold smudged the window with her nose as she peered into the nearby brush. "I told you," she mumbled. "I wasn't paying attention. I was mad at Zane for stealing my bracelet."

"That hardly seems like a good reason for shipping your brother off in the mail."

Marigold sighed. "I knew you wouldn't understand." She was back to fussing with that bracelet. "No one in this family understands anything about me."

Dolores's loose hair tickled her shoulders as she followed the curve of the highway. She let out a sigh of her own. "I know it was an accident, Mari. It's just that you're usually so *responsible*. You know"—Dolores flicked her eyes to the passenger's seat—"I bet I understand more than you think," she said. "I was Fair myself for twenty-seven years."

"Yeah. And now you're not."

"Mari." Dolores tried to make her words soft like butter, so they might actually melt in. "I know it doesn't seem this way to you now, but being Fair is not the end of the world." How many times had Dolores's parents had this same conversation with her when she was Marigold's age? "In some ways"—she paused to turn another corner—"it's actually a gift."

Marigold snorted. "Some gift."

Dolores stamped on the brakes suddenly when a movement

on the side of the road caught her eye, but it was only a deer. She inched the car along at a crawl now, ignoring the annoyed honks of the cars behind her. "Go around!" she shouted at the closed window.

In the passenger's seat, Marigold was silent.

"You know," Dolores told her, "if I'd found my Talent when I was your age, I never would have taken up archaeology."

"But then you *did* find your Talent," Marigold replied. "And aren't you so much happier now?"

Dolores continued to drive.

On and on. On and on. Dolores checked the clock. Forty-five minutes, and still no sign of Will. She fought down the fire that rose in her throat.

"Mom?" Marigold said softly, breaking the worried silence that had been growing between them. "We'll find him. We always find him."

"I just . . ." Dolores blinked, then blinked again. "I don't even know where to look. I feel so . . . useless." A mother should know where to look for her son. A mother should always know.

Marigold set her hands on her knees. "Where would you go if you wanted to get lost?" she asked.

Dolores tightened her mouth into a thoughtful knot. And then, her heart just barely daring to hope, she turned the corner onto River Street.

Zane

ZANE TUGGED OPEN A DRESSER DRAWER AND RIFLED THROUGH the contents. Socks, nothing but socks. He yanked open another. Only sweaters.

Zane could not *believe* Marigold had gone and stuck her nose in his business. What was she thinking, trying to mail his treasures to New Jersey? He'd spent days collecting that stuff, and now Marigold had probably gone and told their mom, and if that were true he'd be in even *more* trouble, especially if his parents ever discovered that he was . . .

WORTHLESS.

Zane slammed the sweater drawer closed and opened another. His only hope now, he reasoned, was to get enough money from Louie to fix the whole apartment. With the bicycle Zane had found parked against the dying hedge outside, he could be at the pawn shop in less than an hour. Sure, he'd have to create a convincing lie about how he came by so much money, but when his parents saw all that cash, they wouldn't question him *too* hard. They'd just be thrilled about how thoughtful their son was, offering up his hard-earned fortune to help the family.

Zane moved on to the closet. Whipped his way through the dress shirts and slacks. He'd thought for sure that Toby would have something worth stealing (the quietest ones, in Zane's experience, always had the best secrets), but it seemed Zane was wrong. There was nothing interesting or valuable in Toby's room. Just some boring old clothes, a neatly made bed, and a half-full glass of water on the nightstand. The only decoration on the plain white walls was a small, sketchy illustration in a black wooden frame.

What a dud.

Zane hoisted the powder blue suitcase to his side and stepped into the hallway.

Had Zane taken a moment to inspect things a little more closely, he would have discovered that there was, in fact, something *quite* interesting about the picture in the black wooden frame.

Beige.

Cracked.

Knobby.

As wide as a rib of celery and as long as a pencil.

On the wall of Toby's bedroom was a framed illustration of Mrs. Asher's hairpin.

The Owner's Peanut Butter Cake With Peanut Butter Frosting

—— a cake that is primarily concerned with peanut butter ——

FOR THE CAKE:

- small sliver of butter (for greasing the cake pan)
- 2 ¼ cups flour (plus extra for preparing the cake pan)
- 1 ½ cups granulated sugar
- 3 ½ tsp baking powder
- 1 tsp salt
- ½ cup creamy peanut butter, at room temperature
- 3 large eggs, at room temperature
- 1 tsp vanilla
- 1 ¼ cups milk, at room temperature

FOR THE FROSTING:

- 3 cups powdered sugar
- ⅔ cup creamy peanut butter, at room temperature
- 1 ½ tsp vanilla
- ½ to ⅔ cup milk

1. Preheat oven to 350°F. Lightly grease the bottoms of two 8-inch round cake pans with butter. Using the cake pans as a template, trace two circles onto wax paper and cut them out, placing one wax circle in the bottom of each pan. Grease

both pans with butter again, covering the wax paper as well as the sides of the pan. Sprinkle the inside of the pans lightly with flour, and tap the pans to distribute it evenly.

2. In a medium bowl, whisk together the flour, granulated sugar, baking powder, and salt, and set aside.

3. In a large bowl, beat the peanut butter and eggs with an electric mixer on medium speed until smooth, about 1 minute. Beat in vanilla and milk until well combined.

4. Gradually add the flour mixture into the peanut butter mixture and beat until combined. Divide the batter between the two cake pans and bake for 30 to 35 minutes, or until a toothpick comes out clean. Cool cakes completely before frosting.

5. While the cakes are cooling, make the frosting: In a medium bowl, cream the powdered sugar and peanut butter with an electric mixer on medium speed until smooth, about 2 or 3 minutes. Add the vanilla and ¼ cup of milk, and beat until well combined. Gradually add more milk, one teaspoon at a time, until the frosting is smooth and spreadable.

6. When the cakes are completely cooled, place one cake layer on a plate and spread a thin layer of frosting on top. Repeat with the second cake layer, and cover the whole cake with frosting.

Cady

THE CAKE CAME TOGETHER QUICKLY. AS CADY SWOOPED THE last curl of peanut butter frosting onto the two-tiered peanut butter cake, she had a whole hour before she and Toby needed to leave for the competition.

She found the Owner slumped at the small desk in the back office, his head in his hands.

"What do you want?" he greeted her.

Cady held out the plate. "I made you some cake."

"Go away."

"I . . ." The cake would make him happy, she knew it would. It was the absolutely perfect cake for him. "I won't leave until you try a bite."

The Owner grabbed the fork from her so suddenly that Cady almost dropped the cake on the floor. He shoveled a bite into his mouth. "Satisfied?" he said, cake crumbs spewing from his lips. "Now get out of here before I—"

His eyes went wide.

"Where did you get the peanut butter to make this cake?" His words were slow, deliberate.

"You like it?" Cady asked hopefully.

"I *said*"—the Owner rose from his chair, his feet two inches above the ground—"where did you get this peanut butter?"

"I . . ." Cady hesitated. No one had ever reacted to one of her cakes quite like this before. "I made it. I found a recipe and I—"

"Show me."

Cady blinked. "Sorry?"

"Show me the recipe you used."

Without another word, Cady pulled the recipe from her pocket. She handed it, wrinkled and brown and fragile, to the Owner. "I only made enough for the cake," she said meekly. "I didn't know you'd want—"

She stopped when she saw the look on his face. It was the sort of look that made Cady feel lit up on the inside. The sort of look people always got when they tried one of her perfect cakes.

She had, without a doubt, made the Owner incredibly happy.

Will

SIR WILL HAD BEEN MARCHING FOR A WHILE. HE GRIPPED his sword—the beige and cracked and knobby one that some might mistake for a precious heirloom, or even a hairpin—and plopped himself down on a rock on the banks of River Street. It was awfully tiring, all this marching, especially when you'd gone and lost one of your shoes. And he missed his trusty steed, Sally. And he hadn't even seen any giants yet. Or monsters. Or cake.

He heard it before he saw it—the loud hissing, like a furious creature sucking in an enormous breath of air. A monster! At last! Sir Will's eyes darted toward the noise.

But it was no monster, only a boring old bus, doing what

boring old buses always did—letting off passengers at the bus stop.

And then off stepped a giant.

"Can I help you, young man?"

To Will's delight, the giant was even more impressive up close. A real-life, humongous giant, *talking* to him. Knots of all sorts poked beneath the bottom edge of the giant's gray suit jacket.

"Young man?"

Will could barely remember how to blink. "I'm on an *adventure*," he breathed. He clutched his hairpin sword a little tighter, wishing Sally were with him.

"Life is the grandest adventure one can go on, isn't it?" the giant said kindly (he seemed to be a very friendly giant). "What else could a person ask for than just to be alive?"

Will knew exactly what else a person could ask for. "Monsters," he said. "And cake."

The giant grinned a sideways sort of grin, a grin that suggested he knew more about the world than he was letting on. "Well," he said slowly, "I don't know about cake, but . . ." This was the part where the giant was going to ask if Will was lost, if it might be a good idea to try to find his parents. Grown-ups were always trying to find Will's parents. "I just so happen to know where there are quite a lot of monsters."

The giant held out his hand, which was nearly as big as Will's head. "Shall I take you?" he asked. "It's near the balloon repair shop, not even a bit out of my way."

Will thought about that, gazing at the man's mammoth hand. His parents had always been very clear that he should never, ever go anywhere with strangers.

But they'd never said anything about giants.

The Owner

FIFTY-THREE YEARS, AND HE'D FINALLY FOUND IT. AS SOON AS he touched the wrinkled brown paper, he knew. *PERFECT PEANUT BUTTER.* His throat tightened at the sight of his mother's loopy scrawl.

The Owner floated to the kitchen, scanning the recipe's ingredients as he went. Peanuts, oil, sugar, salt. Pretty standard stuff. But he supposed that, in the right quantities, any ingredients could be made magical.

Let's see who's the failure now, Dad, he thought as he shouldered open the heavy kitchen door.

Zane

THE HANDLE OF THE POWDER BLUE SUITCASE WAS SLICK IN Zane's hand as he made his way into the last of the upstairs bedrooms, the Owner's. Zane had little hope that the grump of an old man had anything that could earn Zane even a penny, but he was . . .

WORTHLESS.

It couldn't help to look.

Against the far wall sat a single bookshelf, stuffed to the gills with empty jars. Probably two hundred of them at least. Zane took them in. Empty jars wouldn't fetch a lot of money, that was for sure. And they'd be bulky. Hard to carry. But there was something about them . . .

Without knowing precisely why, Zane removed one of the empty jars from the shelf. Studied it.

He was going to need more suitcases.

Will

"HERE WE ARE," THE GIANT TOLD HIM AFTER THEY'D BEEN
walking no more than ten minutes. Will barely even noticed
how sore his left foot was in its muddy sock. It was hard to notice
a thing like that when you were walking with a real live giant.
"And this is where we must part ways, I'm afraid."

"This is where the monsters are?" Will asked.

"All sorts," the giant replied, grinning that sideways grin of
his. "Bony ones, old ones, ones with jaws of massive teeth, some
with fins or fangs or scales."

Will raised his head up, up, up to take in the immensity of the
building before him. Four stories high, shaped from cold gray

stone. At the tippy-top, the building's name was etched in ten-foot-tall block letters.

POUGHKEEPSIE MUSEUM OF NATURAL SCIENCES

Clutching his hairpin sword, Sir Will let go of the giant's hand and stepped across the lawn to continue his adventure.

The Owner

THE OWNER STUCK A TENTATIVE FINGER INTO THE FOOD processor, where his first batch of his mother's peanut butter sat, waiting. He scooped out a mound. It felt crunchy, goopy. Perfect.

Toes tapping anxiously two inches above the floor, the Owner brought the peanut butter to meet his tongue.

And immediately spit it out.

When the food processor hit the wall, the putrid batch of peanut butter splattered. The food processor splintered to bits. The Owner sunk to the floor, chest heaving.

He'd followed the recipe, word for word. And it *was* his mother's recipe, that was certain. The very same one he'd lost on that bus ride fifty-three years ago. But it did not taste anything like the Darlington peanut butter he had loved as a child. It did not taste like happiness. He closed his eyes, letting the truth sink in. It had taken fifty-three years, but finally Mason Darlington Burgess, the good-for-nothing heir to the Darlington fortune, had discovered the secret ingredient to his own mother's peanut butter recipe.

Talent.

His mother had been Talented. All this time, and he'd never known. Nobody had ever known. It was a Talent for churning happiness into her peanut butter that made his mother's results so stupendous. And even Mason Darlington Burgess didn't have a Talent like that in his collection.

He rose to his feet, two inches off the ground.

Mason didn't have the Talent—but he thought he knew who might.

Mrs. Asher's Honey Cake

———— surprisingly spicy for such a sweet cake ————

FOR THE CAKE:

   small sliver of butter (for greasing the cake pan)

   2 ⅓ cups flour (plus extra for preparing the cake pan)

   ½ tsp baking powder

   ½ tsp baking soda

   ¼ tsp salt

   2 ½ tsp cinnamon

   ¼ tsp ground cloves

   ¼ tsp allspice

   ⅔ cup vegetable oil

   ⅔ cup honey

   1 cup granulated sugar

   ⅓ cup brown sugar

   2 large eggs, at room temperature

   ¾ tsp vanilla

   1 cup coffee, at room temperature

   ⅓ cup orange juice, at room temperature

1. Preheat oven to 350°F. Grease two 9-by-5-inch loaf pans with butter. Sprinkle the inside of the pans lightly with flour, and tap the pans to distribute it evenly.

2. In a large bowl, whisk together the flour, baking powder, baking soda, salt, cinnamon, cloves, and allspice.

3. Make a well in the center of the flour mixture and add the vegetable oil, honey, granulated sugar, brown sugar, eggs, vanilla, coffee, and orange juice. Stir with the whisk until well-blended, making sure that no ingredients are stuck to the bottom of the bowl.

4. Distribute the batter evenly between the two pans. Bake for 40 to 50 minutes, or until the tops of the cakes spring back when gently touched in the center. Cool the cakes in the pan for 15 minutes, then turn them out onto a cake rack to cool completely.

Mrs. Asher

THE GUARD AT THE DOOR OF THE POUGHKEEPSIE MUSEUM OF Natural Sciences had seen Will entering through the turnstile. Had assumed he was with the family in front.

The curator of the dinosaur wing had seen him wandering up the stairs to the second floor. Had thought he belonged to the school group.

The second-floor janitor had seen him slouched on a bench outside the archaeology annex. Had figured he must be one of the several tuckered-out grandchildren touring the museum that afternoon.

But all Dolores and Marigold found was one very muddy right shoe.

Dolores sank onto the hard marble bench, a wail caught in her throat. He'd been here, her little boy had been here, but he wasn't here now.

"Mom?" Marigold said, her voice thick with curiosity.

Something underneath the bench caught Dolores's eye. She bent to snatch it up.

It was her hairpin. Beige and cracked and knobby, as wide as a rib of celery and as long as a pencil. She gripped it tight in her hand.

"Mom?" Marigold said again. And she was insistent this time, firm. Dolores looked where her daughter was pointing.

Above them, looming thirty feet high against the wall, was the name of the museum exhibit in which they currently found themselves.

FIFTY YEARS AND COUNTING:
THE SEARCH FOR THE MISSING PIECE

On the banner was an enormous illustration of Mrs. Asher's hairpin.

Toby

HE WAS ARRANGING BOOKS IN THE MYSTERY SECTION OF THE store when the old man stormed up to him.

"Where is she?" he asked Toby. His voice was, if possible, even more of a growl than usual. "Where's the girl?"

"Who, Cady?" Toby placed a book on the shelf between its brothers. "I think she's—" He stopped. Squinted. "Why?" he asked.

"The pathetic little waif is Talented, did you know that?" The Owner flung his arms about as he spoke. "If I had *half* that Talent, I could—"

Toby didn't realize he'd dropped his stack of books until he heard the thud. Didn't realize he'd grabbed the old man by his collar until he felt the icy skin of his neck against his knuckles. "You leave her *alone*," he breathed. Toby's cheeks were hot, burning, the corners of his eyes tense and taut. "Her Talent isn't yours to take, you hear me?"

The Owner let out a chilling laugh. With icy fingers he plucked Toby's hand from his shirt. "You can't protect the girl from everything, Tobias."

Every part of Toby's body burned now, from his heels to his hair. "No," he said, remembering that horrible day in Africa. You certainly couldn't protect anybody from all the terrors of the world. "But I can try."

But the Owner seemed not to hear him. "It could be amazing, you know," he replied, and there was that sparkle in the old man's eye that was as rare as a comet but just as dazzling. "The Darlington Peanut Butter Factory, back in operation. How could you not want to be a part of that?"

Toby studied the man before him. Considered all the thoughts in his head. And when at last he spoke, Toby's words came out like hot oil on a stove—still on the surface, but ready to pop at the slightest disturbance. "Is it so hard to believe that I don't want to be like you?" he said.

They'd leave that hour, Toby decided. That minute. Toby could have his and Cady's meager possessions packed and be out the door in no time, and then Cady would be safe. Toby would explain it all to her after the bakeoff tonight, after Miss

Mallory had declared the trial period officially over. Cady wouldn't want to leave him after that, even if she knew the truth.

He hoped she wouldn't want to leave.

Toby turned on his heel and, half-delirious, left to find Cady.

"You know what your problem has always been, Tobias?" the Owner shouted after him as he crossed the storeroom floor. "You've never been able to admit who you really are."

And a suitcase, Toby thought. He would need to find a suitcase.

Marigold

MARIGOLD SMOOTHED DOWN ONE OF THE THICK, GLOSSY pages of the book she'd bought in the museum gift store—*Fifty Years and Counting: The Search for the Missing Piece*—once more taking in the full-page illustration of her mother's hairpin.

Only it wasn't exactly a hairpin, now was it?

"So you just took this bone?" Marigold asked. Her mother turned another corner on their way back to the Emporium. She was upset about Will, Marigold knew she was upset. But they'd find him. They *always* found him. "This"—Marigold read from the book—"'invaluable piece of paleontological lore'?" Her mother ran her fingers over the hairpin sitting between them on the armrest, as though it were an old friend she was thrilled to see again. But her face was red, just like Will's when he got caught eating too many cookies. "That thing's probably worth thousands of dollars, Mom!"

"Millions."

It was the first word Marigold's mother had uttered since they'd left the museum.

"Well, that's just great, Mom. What am I supposed to do? Turn you in?" Marigold could not believe she was having this conversation with her own mother. "Didn't you teach us not to steal?"

No wonder Zane was turning into such a screwup.

"First of all," Mrs. Asher began, glancing at a flitting motion on the side of the road before continuing, "I didn't steal it. No one but me even knows the thing really exists."

Marigold turned back to the section of the book she'd found earlier. In her best school voice, she read the passage aloud to her mother. "'Over half a century ago, a tremendous paleonto-logical find in Northern Madagascar opened up a new world of research. A nearly complete skeleton was excavated of an extinct bird—the Jupiter bird, it would later be called. At twenty feet tall, the Jupiter bird was the largest bird ever to walk the planet, a marvel of science. Perhaps even more marvelous, however, was the prospect that the Jupiter bird may have had the power of flight, making it by far the largest creature ever to soar in the skies.'" The book went on to say that scientists had been arguing about whether or not the Jupiter bird had been able to fly for over fifty years. They were still arguing today. "'Those who believe that the Jupiter bird did indeed fly say that the answer lies in a single bone—a toe bone, which no one has yet been able to dig up, despite dozens of excavations. If the mythical bone does in fact exist, its discovery would change the face of paleontology—of science—forever.'"

Marigold snapped the book shut.

Her mother pursed her lips together. "So . . . I guess you figured out that the bird could fly."

"*Mom.*"

"Look, I'm not proud of it, all right? I never meant . . ." Mrs. Asher let out a sigh. "You want the whole story?"

Marigold pressed the book against her legs, clammy in their jeans, and nodded.

"Well," her mother began, "it was eleven years ago." She tapped her fingers against the wheel. "When I was in graduate school, interning at the museum. I was there on a scholarship for Fair students." Marigold knew this much of the story already—her mother had always been extremely proud of her work at the museum. "The museum had sponsored a dig in Madagascar for a few months to search for the bone, and I got to go. You remember your father and me telling you about Madagascar?"

Marigold twisted her bracelet around her wrist.

"Anyway," her mother continued, "it was one of the best experiences of my life. I got to work with all of these Talented researchers and paleontologists. Those guys were practically gods to me, and they actually let me dig right in and examine the earth, even though I was Fair. Like I was one of them. I wasn't just one of the volunteers they let tag along to do their grunt work; I was practically a real scientist. I can't tell you how great that felt, after so many years trying to prove myself."

Marigold opened the book again to the illustration of the bone. *The assumed shape of the Jupiter bird's toe bone, as imagined by paleontologists,* the caption read. She looked up at her mother. "So?" she said. "What happened?"

"So." Marigold's mother took a deep breath. "I was pregnant with Zane at the time. Pretty far in. I can't believe I spent all that time digging in the sun with a belly like that, but I was determined." She grinned a little at the memory. "Anyway, because I was pregnant, I had to leave the dig early. The day before I was supposed to leave, the scientists planned a little celebration for me at the site. I was really looking forward to it. Only . . . I didn't get to go. One of the volunteers asked for my help. His wife had died the week before, very suddenly, of pneumonia, and it was all very tragic. He needed help with . . . well, he was going through a rather difficult time. I didn't know him very well, but we'd always been friendly. So I helped him. Missed my own going-away party to do it."

"Mom." This was the way Zane rambled when their parents asked him about his most recent report card. "You were going to tell me about the bone?"

"Ah, yes," Mrs. Asher said. "The bone. Well, maybe it was because I was feeling sad about missing my send-off, I don't know, but whatever the reason, I wanted to see the excavation site one last time before I left. They had regulations about digging hours and solo visitors, but I didn't care. I went, dead of night, just me and a flashlight. It was magical. And I'd only planned to look, really. But . . . well, once I got there, I couldn't help myself. I started to dig."

Marigold didn't realize she'd been leaning forward in her seat while she listened, but she was. Just a tad. She pushed herself back against the headrest. "And you found something," she said.

"Did I ever. Imagine how shocked I was—me, this Talentless little thing, making such a world-changing discovery. It was . . . I can't even describe how amazing that moment felt to me."

For one second, Marigold thought, she really did, that she might know what her mother had felt like, all alone on that dark night in Madagascar. It might feel a bit like playing the oboe, when the notes came out exactly perfect and tickled your lips and wrapped themselves around your body and danced through your hair . . . right before you went sour on the C sharp for the eightieth time.

"Anyway, I must've been at the site longer than I'd thought," her mother went on, "because soon enough your father was there in a panic, telling me we had to rush to the airport to catch our flight. I didn't even have time to tell anyone about this incredible discovery I'd made. And I thought—I guess it was silly, but I thought at the time I'd just tell them later, when I got back home. So I slipped the bone into my pocket. I didn't even tell your father I'd found it, because . . . I think I simply wanted to hold on to that feeling a little longer, this knowledge that I had. Me, the only person in the entire world."

"Dad doesn't know?" Marigold asked. "Even now?" Her mother shook her head. "But why didn't you ever tell anyone?"

"I kept meaning to. Always thought I would. But one day went by, and I thought, 'Let me just keep this feeling a little longer. One more day.' And then another day went by, and another. Then I found out they replaced me at the museum, with this Talented fellow from Romania. Only until my maternity leave was up, that's what they said. But I knew they didn't want me back. Why would they want *me* when they could have someone like that? You should have seen all the papers he'd written!"

"But if you'd *told* them about the bone," Marigold said, "then they would've taken you back in a heartbeat." It was like trying to talk sense into Zane, she thought, or scolding a bad puppy.

Her mom simply shrugged. "Maybe they would have," she replied. "Or maybe they would've been furious at me for keeping it from them for so long, and the credit would have gone to someone else."

"But you don't *know* that's what would've—"

"I was a pregnant, Untalented young woman," her mother said, and she sounded much more serious now. Much more like her old self. "I have a pretty good idea of how things would have gone."

"But—"

"Anyway, that's the story, really. The days turned into weeks, and then months, and I never told anybody. I took up knitting to bide my time waiting for your brother to arrive, and we all know how that turned out. One day your father saw the toe bone on our nightstand and asked what it was, and I told him it was a hairpin. He never even batted an eye."

Marigold looked at her mother's face as they turned onto Argyle Road, beginning the long, wooded stretch that would lead them back to the Emporium. And for the first time, Marigold felt like she was really seeing her. Her high cheekbones, her mischievous eyes. Her mother had had a whole life before Marigold and her brothers were even a thought in her head. Marigold had always known that, of course, but now . . .

"You're going to tell them now, right?" Marigold asked her. "At the museum? You're going to tell them about the bone?"

Her mother thought about it.

What was there to *think* about?

"*Mom?*"

"I know I should, but—"

"Mom!" Marigold slapped at her knees so hard, the book

tumbled to the floor. "You *have* to. You know that's the right thing to do. Aren't you always telling us to do the right thing?" Marigold didn't like the feeling that had developed in her stomach—the feeling like she was being more of a mother than her mother was. "You know Principal Piles wants Zane to go to boarding school next year?" Marigold hadn't planned on ratting out her brother, but her mother had to know. She had to understand that there were *consequences* when you acted—hadn't her parents always said there would be *consequences*? "She sent you a letter, but you haven't even read it. He's in trouble, Mom. He gets in trouble all the time, and don't you think he needs a good examp—"

Mrs. Asher stopped the car. Pushed her foot to the brake, right there in the middle of Argyle Road.

"Mom?"

She leaned over Marigold and flipped open the door to the glove compartment, took out an envelope, and handed it to Marigold. Then she shut the door again and returned her gaze out the windshield.

It was the letter from the school, about Zane. And it was open.

"You read it?" Marigold asked. Her mother nodded. "But what are you and Dad going to—"

Her mother ran her fingers over the bone between them on the armrest. "Your father and I are still deciding. We haven't talked to Zane yet." When Marigold's eyes went huge, her mother continued on. "I know Zane has trouble sometimes in school, but that doesn't mean—"

"He doesn't *have* trouble, Mom. He *is* trouble."

"And you think boarding school will help all that?"

Marigold puffed out a lungful of air. She didn't answer, even as her mother took back the letter, returned it to the glove compartment, and started back down the road. They remained silent, both of them, even as they pulled into the parking lot in front of the Lost Luggage Emporium.

The truth was, Marigold didn't know if boarding school would help her delinquent brother any more than she knew if she'd find her Talent in a day or a year or never. How could she know something like that? But what she did know was that her brother had broken the rules—he broke the rules all the time—and Principal Piles had *said* he should go to boarding school. And Marigold knew—she'd been told her whole life—that if you did something wrong, you should be punished for it. (Shouldn't you?) And if you tried really hard at something, you should be rewarded. (Right?)

Marigold stepped out of the car, clutching the museum book tight to her chest.

"Mari?"

She turned around to look at her mother again. She looked older than usual, with streaks of gray in her hair that Marigold had somehow never noticed before.

"I just need time to think, okay?" Marigold nodded slowly as her mother put the car into reverse. "Keep an eye out in case Will comes back here."

Marigold shut the door, and her mother backed out of the parking lot, continuing her hunt for the youngest Asher child.

Neither of them noticed the ferret scrambling up the roof of Mrs. Asher's car.

V

When the curly-haired girl found her, V was sitting on the girl's perfectly made bed, playing her oboe. There was something about the expressive ups and downs of the music—the fluid emotion that escaped with every twitch of V's fingers—that V couldn't pull herself away from. But the girl didn't seem to mind. She simply flopped herself down sideways on the bed, a book slapped over her stomach, and let V play.

A noise in the doorway distracted V from her music for a moment. The young man who ran errands for the owner of the building was standing in the hallway, one powder blue suitcase in each hand. He stopped to ask the curly-haired girl a question, his voice tilting up at the edge of his words—with tension or hurry, V could not be sure. The girl raised herself on her elbows to answer him, and as she did, the book on her stomach shifted ever so slightly. And then the most curious thing happened.

When the man spied the book, his face . . . *changed.*

It only lasted a moment, no more than a blink, but V was sure of it. For one fraction of an instant, the man in the doorway had been a different person. The outer edges of his eyebrows had turned up, just a touch. His usually straight nose had tilted to a crooked angle. And his normally flat hair had developed a hint of a cowlick.

The man was a chameleon.

When the curly-haired girl left the room not two minutes later for some task or another, V scooped the glossy white book off the bed. V was curious to know what could possibly make a man so excited that he revealed his true self, a self he clearly wanted to keep hidden.

It seemed to be a book about some sort of archaeological excavation. There were photographs of people digging, people scraping dirt off of bones. V flipped to a page filled with photos of men and women of all sorts holding shovels and smiling. It was a generally unremarkable book.

And then V noticed one particular fist-size photo in the bottom left corner that, for just a moment, elbowed all thoughts of the chameleon clean out of her head. It couldn't be. It just . . . couldn't.

It was.

She studied the photo more closely, and as she did, the thoughts of the chameleon trickled back into her brain. V scrambled to the window, where she could just make out the chameleon, tossing his two blue suitcases into the back of his pickup truck. He covered them quickly with a wrinkled brown tarp, then called across the parking lot to the tiny black-haired girl.

With two sharp *shrick-shricks*, V ripped the photo out of the book. She tucked it in her pocket. And, as fast as her two old legs could carry her, she hurried down the stairs.

Cady

THERE WAS AN ODD SORT OF CLATTER FROM THE TRUCK BED AS Cady piled into the car to join Toby, but when they checked in the mirrors, neither saw anything more than the brown tarp that Toby kept there to cover suitcases.

"Probably just a squirrel or something," Toby declared.

"Aren't we leaving a little earlier than we planned?" Cady asked as Toby turned the key in the ignition.

Toby shook his head. "You never know how much traffic there will be, and parking's always a disaster. Better early than late, that's what I always say." And he gave her a smile. It seemed off, somehow, but Cady wasn't quite sure why.

The Owner

BRRRING! THE PHONE CLATTERED ON ITS STAND. **BRRRING!**

The Owner hadn't noticed the missing truck until it had been far too late to catch them. What an imbecile Toby was. *Brrring!* Couldn't he see what a gift he'd been given in that girl? *Brrring!* The Owner would find them. *Brrring!* He was frustrated, but not worried. *Brrring!* Now that he knew the Talent existed, he would find a way to get it. *Brrring!* It was only a matter of time until he—

Brr—!

"*What?*" the Owner snapped into the receiver, breaking off the phone midsqueal. "What could possibly be so important that a person could let the phone ring twenty-seven times?"

"I . . ." The voice on the other end was meek, kind. A young woman. "I'm so sorry to bother you," she said. "I'm Jennifer Mallory, from the orphanage. I was looking for Cadence."

"Get in line," the Owner replied. And he had almost succeeded in slamming down the phone when he heard the muffled words on the other end. "What did you say?" he asked, returning the receiver to his ear.

"I only wondered," the woman repeated, "if Cady and Toby had left for the convention center yet."

Will

WILL STOOD IN HIS MUDDY SOCKS ON THE LOWEST STEP OF THE
Poughkeepsie train station, pressing his hands into his ears as
the train screeched to a noisy stop. He had (as usual) been fol-
lowing his nose toward an adventure, and (as usual) he couldn't
quite remember the route his nose had taken him on. What
Will did know was that it had been an amazing day—*giants!
monsters!*—and that all he needed to make his adventure complete was an enormous helping of cake.

Will looked down at his feet. He wiggled his cold, damp toes
inside his cold, damp socks.

It turned out that adventure was a tiring thing. Will's feet
were sore, his bones were exhausted, and he missed Sally

something awful. Even if he *did* find some cake, what good would it be without Sally there to enjoy it with him?

Click-click-clack!

Will perked up his ears. There was a sound from the train that sounded suspiciously like—

Click-click-clack!

"Sally!" Will leapt up the stairs and, with the ease of somebody who has been losing himself in curious places for six long years, Will—*click-click-clack!*—slunk his way aboard the train. He followed Sally's chattering—*click!*—through the lunch car—*click!*—past the luggage compartment—*clack!*—and down the main aisle.

"All aboard! Last stop New York City!"

Click-click-clack!

"Sally!" he cried, squeezing himself through to the next car. "Hold on, I'm almost—"

Click!

Will came to a halt. It was not Sally making the noise: Sally was nowhere to be seen.

"Ticket please, ma'am."

Click-click!

It was the train conductor, snipping holes in the tickets of each passenger as he passed through the aisle. He reached for the ticket of the woman in the nearest seat, who—based on the numerous crossword puzzles scattered around her—appeared to be a Talented solver. "You'll need a ticket for your son as well," the conductor told her, nodding his head at Will, gaping in the aisle.

"Oh, he's not my—"

But Will had vanished. As the train lurched to a start, Will tucked himself neatly into an overhead luggage rack and curled into a tight ball, doing his best to rub some warmth into his muddy toes. He hadn't found Sally, and he hadn't found the end of his adventure, either.

Will sniffled. For the first time in his life, he thought he just might be lost.

Cady

THE CONVENTION CENTER IN NEW YORK CITY WAS EVEN MORE swarming than last year. Everywhere Cady looked there were bakers and their guests, dashing from here to there, clanging cake pans together and hollering about butter. WELCOME TO THE FIFTY-THIRD SUNSHINE BAKERS OF AMERICA ANNUAL CAKE BAKEOFF! a silver banner greeted them.

Toby gripped her hand tightly. "Good thing we got here early," he said, his gaze traveling down the long rows of baking stations in the center of the room, where the contestants would be competing. Volunteers were bustling with last-minute preparations, checking to be sure that each station had the same ingredients in the same amounts, wiping down the counters, preheating the ovens. A man with hair as slick as a pregreased cake pan pushed an enormous flour barrel on a wheeled platform to fill the smaller containers at each station. He didn't seem to be paying much attention to his job. His nose was buried deep in a copy of *Face Value*, even as he walked, so that he spilled more flour than not.

Cady searched the crowd. Whispers from admiring fans seemed to be echoing off the walls. "There she is, that's the little orphan!" "Look, it's Cadence! She'll win again this year for sure." But no matter how many people seemed to know her, none of them was Miss Mallory.

She'll come, Cady assured herself. *Miss Mallory will come, and she'll declare the adoption official, and that will be that.*

Cady led Toby toward someone who looked like she might be in charge—a very large lady, wearing a tall white chef's hat—wondering if everybody's stomachs churned so much inside them right before they got everything they'd ever wanted.

Marigold

It was late afternoon when Marigold finally got a chance to squeeze in some Talent-hunting. Cady had already left for the bakeoff, so Marigold was all by her lonesome, out in the wooded spot where Argyle Road met the main highway. (It was a good place for Talent-hunting, Marigold had discovered, because there was no one to bother her but a few squirrels.) The air was still as Marigold tried one Talent after another, making her way slowly down her list. Yodeling. No. Standing on one foot. No. Hopping from tree to tree. (Ouch.) No. Marigold tightened her bracelet more securely around her wrist and pressed on, stretching her toes to their tippy-tips and arching her arms above her head to figure out if her Talent was ballet dancing.

"Maybe you have a Talent for farting. You've always seemed especially good at that."

"Zane!" Marigold slapped her hands to her sides and whirled around. Sure enough, there was her delinquent older brother, perched atop a bicycle that most certainly didn't belong to him. Attached to the back by a short length of rope was Zane's skateboard, piled high with four powder blue suitcases strapped down tight, each one stuffed to bursting. "Off to Louie's to sell some more stuff you stole?" Marigold sneered, hands on her hips.

"What do you care?" Zane replied, pressing his bike forward.

Marigold cut him off, gripping her fists around Zane's handlebars. "I care because you tried to steal *my* bracelet." From far down the wooded road, Marigold could hear the sound of a car, someone leaving the Emporium, but she didn't move an inch. If she did, Zane would zoom right by her, and then he'd *never* learn his lesson. "You can't just *do* stuff like that, Zane." Now the squirrels seemed to be interested in what was happening in the road. A few of them began inching their way out to the dirt path, *yut-yut-yut*ing as they sniffed at Zane's tires.

Zane tried to jerk his handles away. "I never stole your stupid bracelet," he said.

Marigold clutched the handlebars, anger radiating from her knuckles. "So you're a liar now, too?" she spat. "No wonder you have to go to boarding school."

Zane jerked his handles again, harder this time. "Shut *up*," he snapped. "Mari the Middling."

With a rage that welled up from deep inside her, Marigold pushed her brother and the bicycle, hard, backward down the path . . .

. . . straight into the oncoming car.

V

V COULDN'T QUITE SAY WHAT HAD COMPELLED HER TO LEAP into the back of that truck (not that she could say much of anything). She didn't know where the chameleon was going, or what she planned on doing when she came face-to-shifting-face with him. Perhaps this chameleon was nothing like the one who had charmed her Caroline right out from underneath her. Perhaps Caroline hadn't needed much charming to begin with. But what if V could have stopped it all if she'd only *said* something? What if, by exposing *this* chameleon, V could stop a similar mother from experiencing a similar heartache?

She had to try.

V smoothed her hand over the photograph she'd ripped from

the book, the faces tinted lightly brown from the sun shining through the tarp above. Three people, working on an archaeological dig in the blazing sun, smiling together for the camera.

The mother.

The father.

A baby girl.

V clutched the photograph to her chest with one hand, sloughing her way out from under the tarp with the other. She lifted herself from the truck bed and did her best to take in her surroundings.

The convention center. The chameleon had driven them to the convention center in New York City. V knew the towering glass building well. She'd given many talks here in her time. V followed the stream of visitors in chef's hats and colored aprons, some toting cake pans under their arms, others simply fidgeting nervously.

V snuck her way through the side entrance, past a greasy-haired young gentleman pushing an enormous barrel of flour. (The man was too engrossed in his book to notice her entrance, which V supposed she should take as a compliment.) She steadied herself, taking one last look at the photograph for courage, then—bumping only slightly against the flour barrel as she nudged past—V made her way inside.

She did not, at that moment, realize that she'd dropped the photograph.

Mrs. Asher

WHAT DOLORES HAD BEEN HOPING FOR WHEN SHE ROLLED down the window was a breath of fresh air. A bit of a country breeze to help clear her head as she continued down the highway.

What she got was a faceful of ferret.

"Aaaaaagggggggghhhhhh!" Dolores screeched, swerving as she struggled with the furry blob that had attached itself to her nose. She finally managed to pull to the side of the road and wrestle the critter to her lap. "Sally!" she cried, willing her heart to slow to only three hundred beats per second. "Where on earth did you—You scared me half to—Oh, Sally." Dolores's voice softened as the ferret curled into a frightened, hairy ball and sniffled a sad sort of sniffle. "You miss him, too, don't you?"

Click-click-clack, Sally replied.

Dolores scratched at the scruff of Sally's neck. "Where in the world could that boy be? I bet *you'd* know"—*scratch, scratch, scratch*—"since you and Will are always going on all those adven—"

Dolores stopped talking. Slowly, with one hand still around the ferret in her lap, she returned her foot to the gas pedal and eased back onto the highway.

Zane

IT WAS A CURIOUS SENSATION, BEING HIT BY AN ONCOMING CAR while flying backward on a bicycle. Somehow thrilling and terrifying both at once. Like a roller coaster, but without a safety bar.

The part after the collision, where Zane flew feet-over-face past his handlebars and thwacked headfirst into the dirt, that wasn't thrilling at all.

There was a screech of tires and the slam of a car door.

"You damn kids!" came a voice behind him.

Marigold rushed to Zane, picking his head out of the dirt. "Oh, Zane, I'm so sorry, are you okay?" Zane was not okay. His whole head throbbed, his palms were burning. He wondered if he might have broken an ankle.

"You *damn kids*!" came the voice again. The Owner. "Move this mess, *now*!"

As Zane did his best to rub the sting out of the back of his neck, Marigold stood to her full height, hands on her hips. "You *hit* my *brother*!" she screeched. Dozens of squirrels, Zane noticed as his vision began to clear, had leapt out from the trees, and they were swarming into the road in order to . . .

Actually, what *were* they doing? Zane craned his neck ever so slightly, pins and needles soaring up his spine as he did so, to take in the scene.

A mangled bicycle. Four suitcases burst open in the dirt. Cameras, wallets, belt buckles. And jars. There were jars everywhere, scattered across the road. Broken and cracked and slivered, every last one. And rising up from the shards of each broken jar—Zane blinked when he saw it—was a fine sort of mist. A gray haze that swirled up into the sky, slowly at first, then swaying slightly with the breeze until it funneled up, up, up into the clouds.

Yut!

Yut!

The squirrels seemed fascinated, digging their curious faces right down into the broken glass to sniff.

Yut yut! Yutyutyutyutyut!

The Owner had noticed the mess, too. And he wasn't as happy about it as the squirrels.

"You *damn kids*!" he screamed again. His face was purple, veins bulging in his forehead. With two burly hands, he lifted the twisted heap of a bicycle off the ground and threw it into the bushes. A pedal caught Marigold in the cheek, and she squawked in surprise, slapping her hand to cover it.

But Zane had already seen the blood forming.

"You leave my sister alone!" he howled, rising, teetering to his feet. Zane's ankle wailed at him to stay still, his hands hollered, his knees shrieked, but Zane didn't listen. He lunged at the Owner, sending the squirrels chittering in all directions.

Things became a bit of a blur after that. Maybe it was because Zane was in so much pain that he found it hard to follow the events that unfolded right in front of him. But what *seemed* to happen (although it couldn't be what *really* happened, because it was all too peculiar to be true) was that something in the Owner's pocket let out a soft *plunk!*, like a pebble being tossed to the floor, and the Owner suddenly shrunk two inches. And then, without warning, there was a sharp chill in Zane's forehead. He couldn't tell if it lasted a moment or a lifetime, but it was . . . *cold.*

And then, all at once, the Owner shoved Zane back into the dirt.

In the Owner's hand was a small rock of ice.

Cady

"**AND WHAT CAKE WILL YOU BE BAKING TODAY?**" THE LARGE woman with the chef's hat asked Cady.

"Hmm?" Cady looked up from her baking station, just as the man with the greasy black hair wheeled by with his flour barrel. Nose still in his book, he scooped a mound of flour from the barrel into Cady's container. She coughed out a bit of flour dust.

"Your cake," the woman said again. She tapped the clipboard in her hand. "I have to write it down, what you'll be baking."

"Oh, I . . ." Cady looked up into the bleachers, where the rows and rows of guests were sitting. She couldn't spot Toby, but she knew he was there somewhere. Miss Mallory would be, too, soon. *Probably the last time I'll ever see her*, Cady thought.

She turned back to the woman with the clipboard. "I don't know," she said at last. "I usually wait until I meet the judge." How could Cady bake the perfect cake for the judge until she knew who that judge was?

The woman frowned. "Well, the judges will be coming out to greet the contestants in a moment, but I really do need to note down—"

"Judges?" Cady asked.

"Yes." Cady could tell by the woman's voice that she was growing more and more impatient. "They've changed the rules around a little bit since last time. There are five judges this year."

Cady's eyes went wide. "*Five?* But how am I supposed to . . . ?"

The woman's face softened just the slightest. "You're never going to be able to please every person every time," she told Cady.

Cady squinted her eyes shut for a short second, searching her brain. The large woman standing before her was, surprisingly, not a cake at all, but rather a blackberry pie. Her eyes snapped open. If only she were baking for *this* woman, she'd have won the trophy already.

The woman glanced down the long row of bakers. "Look, take a minute to think about it, all right? I'll come back to you last. But if I might make a suggestion"—she regarded Cady kindly—"why don't you bake the cake that's *your* favorite?"

Cady kicked her toe against the oven door as the woman in the chef's hat continued on down the row. *Bake the cake that's your favorite.* It sounded so simple. But how was Cady supposed to know what her favorite cake was? Cherry? Chocolate? Almond? Cady had never thought she'd have to worry about such a thing until her Adoption Day party and, for some reason, when she squeezed shut her eyes and searched her brain, all she found was a mess of confusion. But somewhere, out in the audience, Toby and Miss Mallory would be watching, and Cady didn't want to disappoint them.

Cady set her elbows on the countertop and did her best to think. She was so busy with her own fitful thoughts that she didn't notice the small fist-size slip of paper that had found its way into her flour bin.

Marigold

MARIGOLD WAS TYPICALLY THE TYPE OF GIRL WHO REFRAINED from whacking surly old men in the shins as hard as she could. But today was not a typical day.

Whack! "You hurt my brother!" Marigold screamed at the Owner. *Whack!* When he tried to push her away, she jumped on his back and—*whack!*—kicked him even harder. Zane was still in the dirt, moaning. *Whack!* "You *hurt* him!"

"Get off, get *off*!" The Owner raised a hand—was that an *ice cube* inside it?—to push Marigold away, but she was too quick for him. She whacked his arm, hard as she could, in the elbow, so that he shrieked and convulsed.

The ice cube snaked down his arm and found its way to

Marigold's wrist, where it promptly wedged itself under her Talent bracelet. She squealed at the sudden chill of it, trying to shake the frosty stone from her skin, even as she clutched tight to the Owner's back. But the ice cube was trapped beneath the three shiny silver beads of Marigold's bracelet, and she could only watch, mesmerized, as it quickly shrunk—tiny, tinier, tiniest—into her skin, the cold traveling through her veins, up her arm, and into her chest. And just like that, the icy stone was gone, vanished, sunk completely inside her.

The Owner tossed Marigold to the ground, where she landed—*thump*—next to Zane. Spinning on his heel, the Owner crackled across the broken mounds of glass, flung himself inside his car, and left in a screech of tires and dust.

"What . . ." Marigold rubbed her wrist as the Owner's car disappeared down the main highway. "What happened?"

"I think . . ." Zane said slowly, rubbing at his forehead. He frowned. "I think you got my Talent."

"*What?*" Marigold wouldn't have believed it for a second if she didn't feel the overwhelming desire to hock a loogie right that very moment. She kicked a shard of broken jar across the Owner's tire tracks, sending the last squirrel sprinting back into the bushes. "We should go to the police," she said, doing her best to think things through. "That guy's dangerous. He just *stole* your *Talent*, so who *knows* what he . . ." She trailed off with the immensity of it all.

Zane pulled his hand from his forehead to blow cool air onto his scraped-up palms. "You're right," he said between breaths.

Marigold snapped her head up. Of all the startling things that had happened that afternoon, those two words were perhaps the most extraordinary. "I am?"

"Yeah," Zane said. "We *should* go to the police. But how are we supposed to get there?"

That's when the rope dropped from the sky, a thick length of rope with knots tied into it, expertly, every foot or so. Marigold and Zane's eyes followed the whole length of it, up, up, up, until they found the source—one hundred feet above them in the sky.

A hot air balloon, with a red-and-blue striped top. It looked surprisingly like the balloon that had crashed into their apartment wall only one week ago.

A man leaned over the edge of the basket to peer down at them. Marigold could just make out the top of his gray suit.

"You kids need a lift?" he called down.

Toby

TOBY CHECKED HIS WATCH. GLANCED AT CADY WITH HER elbows on the floury countertop, and then checked his watch again. He might have outfoxed the Owner for the moment, but that greasy-haired fool with his book was making Toby nervous. What if someone figured out the truth about Toby before he had a chance to explain it to Cady for himself? He would feel much more at ease when this whole event was over.

Toby checked his watch again.

Zane's Garlic Cake

— a cake that's not as terrible as it seems, on the surface, to be —

FOR THE CAKE:

- 6 tbsp butter (plus extra for greasing the cake pan)
- 5 cloves garlic, finely minced
- 1 ¼ cups flour (plus extra for preparing the cake pan)
- 1 ½ tsp baking powder
- ½ tsp salt
- ½ cup Parmesan cheese, finely grated
- ⅛ tsp black pepper
- 3 large eggs, yolks and whites separated, at room temperature
- 1 tbsp honey
- ¾ cup milk, at room temperature

1. Preheat oven to 375°F. Grease an 8-inch round cake pan with butter, and flour lightly.

2. In a small saucepan, melt the butter over low heat. When butter is fully melted, add the minced garlic and cook, stirring, until slightly fragrant, about 1 minute. Remove from heat and allow to cool.

3. In a large bowl, whisk together the flour, baking powder, salt, Parmesan, and pepper, until well combined. Set aside.

4. In a small bowl, mix together the three egg yolks, the honey, and the milk. Pour this mixture into the flour mixture, and stir until well combined. Gradually add the cooled garlic mixture, and stir until well combined. Set aside.

5. In a clean small bowl, beat the three egg whites with an electric mixer on high speed until stiff peaks form, about 3 to 5 minutes. Carefully fold the egg whites into the rest of the batter, until just combined.

6. Spoon the batter into the pan, and bake for 25 to 30 minutes, until the cake is golden brown and the surface feels firm to the touch. Serve warm or cold, cut into wedges.

Zane

"THIS IS *AMAZING*," MARIGOLD COOED, BENT FAR OVER THE edge of the hot air balloon basket, watching the trees zoom by below. She was difficult to hear over the roaring propane valve above their heads, but Zane heard her anyway.

"Will you sit down already?" he grumbled, scooching his butt farther against the padded seat. Zane had not wanted to board this stupid aircraft. He had *not*. As soon as he'd seen the giant red-and-blue striped balloon, he'd known it was a bad idea. It could crash at any moment, for one thing. But what was Zane supposed to do once Marigold started shimmying up that rope? He couldn't very well let her fly off by herself. He rubbed his forehead, but the chill would not come out. "You're gonna fall," he called over to her, "and then Mom and Dad will probably blame *me*."

The man in the gray suit leaned closer to Zane, one thick-gloved hand still resting on the knob of the propane valve. Zane had been watching the man work the balloon's controls ever since they'd climbed inside the basket, and he was good at it. Skilled. The kind of man who should be able to maneuver himself and his hot air balloon out of any danger that came his way.

Including a spit attack from an eleven-year-old boy out a twelfth-floor window.

"Everything okay with you, young man?" the man in the gray suit asked.

Zane shot a glance across the basket toward Marigold, but she wasn't paying them any mind. She was busy using her new Talent to spit at treetops zooming past. Good for her. What had Zane ever used his Talent for, anyway, besides busting giant holes in his family's apartment wall?

WORTHLESS.

"What did you say?" the man in the gray suit asked.

Zane shot his head up. Had he said that out loud?

"Nothing," he muttered.

The man in the gray suit fiddled with the valve knobs, checked his gauges and, when he seemed satisfied with their current position and direction, left his post to take a seat next to Zane.

"I'm not upset, if that's what you're worried about," he told Zane.

Zane squinted at him. He knew it was only a matter of time before this man recognized him as the kid who'd wrecked his balloon. But he'd never hoped to dream that—

"It was an old bicycle, anyway," the man in the gray suit went on. "And I'm the one who forgot it there, so really I can't be upset that it got smashed."

"Oh." Zane kept his eyes on one of the trees in the distance, a fir. "Well, good."

From practically the moment he was born, Zane realized, he'd been ruining things. He'd ruined his chances of being a good student, he'd ruined his family's apartment. He couldn't even get a bunch of junky old jars to a pawn shop without ruining them. Maybe Principal Piles was right. Maybe he should go to boarding school. Maybe he *was* worthless.

The man in the gray suit gazed out at the horizon. "It's an awful shame about all those Talents, though."

Zane watched as the brown tip-top of the fir tree bobbed ever closer. "What Talents?" he asked the man.

"Your collection. In the jars. I was sorry to see them all escape like that."

"*That* was what was in those jars?" Zane shrieked. He'd had four entire *suitcases* full of Talents and he went and ruined those, too? Those would've raked in a *fortune* at Louie's.

189

"No question," the man said. He let out a shallow snort. "There are some Talented squirrels out in the woods tonight. That'd be a sight, huh?"

Despite himself, Zane laughed. "Yeah," he said. "I guess so."

The balloon bobbed and weaved with the air currents for a while, the patches of trees making way for taller and taller buildings, and Zane sat, not thinking much of anything.

Trying hard not to think much of anything.

WORTHLESS.

"If you don't mind my asking," the man in the gray suit piped up after several minutes of silence, "what were you doing with all of those jars, anyway? If you didn't know what was in them?"

Zane studied the laces of his shoes, the way they crossed each other. Over and under and over and under. "I was going to try to sell them." His voice was low beneath the roar of the flame, but the man in the gray suit seemed to hear him fine. "I thought I could get a couple bucks for them. I needed the money to help my parents." Over and under and over and under. "Our apartment . . ." He let out a huff of a breath. "They need to fix our apartment, and I thought I could help."

The man in the gray suit nodded thoughtfully. "But those jars, they weren't yours to sell. You stole them."

Zane scrunched his eyes closed. *Worthless worthless worthless.* He'd wrecked the apartment with his stupid Talent. *Worthless.* He'd tried to fix it. *Worthless.*

"Do you know why human beings need to spit?" the man in the gray suit asked suddenly.

Zane popped his eyes open. "Huh?"

The man pointed a finger at Marigold, still hunched over the side of the basket, practicing her new Talent. "It's mucus," he said. "Your body builds up mucus, which is teeming with bacteria, which can cause your body harm. So we spit."

Zane raised an eyebrow.

"If you think about it," the man went on, "spitting is a beautiful thing. Healthy. It's just that it can sometimes take a bad direction. It might, for instance," the man said, brushing a speck of dust from one of his gloves, "be shot at a person as he was piloting his hot air balloon. That would not only be unhealthy, but downright dangerous."

Zane's eyes went wide. "I'm—I'm sorry," he stuttered. "I—I never meant—"

To Zane's surprise, the man in the gray suit chuckled. "Don't worry, young man, I'm not angry," he said. "I was flying much too close to your building in any case, and I survived the crash without a scratch, now didn't I?"

"But I really didn't—"

The man stood up, cutting Zane's thought in half. "I think," he told him, "that you are a young man with very good intentions." He lifted his hand up to the propane valve and tweaked the knob. "Healthy." He tweaked it a little more. "But perhaps you sometimes shoot in the wrong direction."

Zane thought about that. "I'm still sorry," he said. "I shouldn't have done it."

The man grinned a sideways sort of grin. It was a grin that suggested he knew more about the world than he was letting on. "I appreciate that," he told Zane. And then he lifted up both gloved hands and fiddled with the valves until the balloon made a steep descent.

Marigold whirled around. The cut on her cheek had stopped bleeding, but the skin was still red, swollen. "What's going on?" she asked.

The man in the gray suit pulled his hands from the knobs. "We've reached our destination," he announced cheerfully.

Zane peered down over the edge of the basket, where the expansive glass walls of the New York City convention center gleamed in the sunshine. "That's not the police station," he said. "This is Cady's cake contest." Even from here, Zane could make out the enormous banner: WELCOME TO THE FIFTY-THIRD SUN-SHINE BAKERS OF AMERICA ANNUAL CAKE BAKEOFF!

The man in the gray suit began uncoiling the thick length of knotted rope from the corner of the basket. "Well, ballooning is not an exact science, you know. Besides, you might be needed here."

"Needed?" Marigold asked.

The man in the gray suit whipped the rope over the side of the basket, where it unfurled to the sidewalk below with a loud *fwop!*

"This is where your ride ends, I'm afraid," the man informed them. "It's been a pleasure having you both aboard."

"What did you mean, *needed*?" Marigold asked again.

"Let me help you down."

Zane waited until Marigold had both feet safely on the ground before he hoisted his leg over the edge of the basket, clinging tight to the rope. Every inch of his body was still angry at him after his run-in with the Owner. Zane took a deep breath, focused his eyes on his fingers, and began his descent.

"Young man?" The man in the gray suit leaned over the basket.

"Yeah?" Zane said.

"I would advise you not to worry so much. I'm sure your next year at McDermott Elementary will go much more smoothly than the last."

Zane tensed the toes of his sneakers tight against the rope. "Actually," he said, his throat doing its best to catch at the words as he spoke them, "I don't think I'm going back. My parents are probably going to send me to—" He paused. "How did you know I go to McDermott?"

The man in the gray suit frowned. "Didn't you mention? Somehow I thought you had. No matter. When I read in the paper today about the preparations your new principal was making for the school's—"

For just one moment, Zane thought his fingers might lose their grip on the rope. "*New* principal?" he said.

———

"Hadn't you heard?" the man in the gray suit replied. "It seems the school's last principal was deemed—how was it phrased?—'unfit to head the school.'"

At that, Zane smiled. He looked down the length of rope once more to the sidewalk, where Marigold was waving at him. "Maybe it won't be such a bad year after all."

"I have a feeling, in fact," the man in the gray suit told him, leaning farther over the basket to talk to Zane in conspiratorial tones, "that you might just find it to be very . . . worthwhile."

Miss Mallory

"Ma'am, I'm sorry, but I simply can't let you in without a ticket. In any case, the competition is already well under way."

Miss Mallory sucked in her breath at the large woman in the chef's hat who was too busy *ma'am*ing her to listen to what she had to say. She had gotten to the convention center much later than she'd planned, due to an unprecedented traffic jam on the highway. She'd tried to tune in to the radio to see what was causing the delay, but all she'd gotten was nonsense about an influx of Talented squirrels, stopping traffic with their amazing acrobatics and unnatural abilities. Apparently there was even one squirrel who could whistle.

"I told you"—Miss Mallory kept her voice calm—"I can't find

my ticket. I must have lost it somehow. But my contestant is inside. And it's very important that I—"

"The contestant's name?" the woman asked drily, eyes scrolling her clipboard.

"Cadence," Miss Mallory replied. "Right there." She pointed. "See?"

"Yes, I do," the woman answered. She flicked her eyes up to meet Miss Mallory's. "And I also see that Ms. Cadence already has one guest inside and has not marked down that she's expecting another. Now unless you can produce your ticket, I'm afraid I must insist you leave."

"I *told* you," Miss Mallory said again, patting her pockets to see if perhaps the ticket had hidden itself inside.

She did not finish the sentence.

There was a tug in her chest just as she reached her hand into her pocket. It was not an especially strong tug, and it was not the sort of tug that Miss Mallory usually felt with her orphans. But it was a tug all the same.

From her pocket, Miss Mallory produced the black ceramic bird, the one she'd found in the suitcase in the woods. She regarded it in her hand a moment.

"Is this yours?" she asked the woman in the chef's hat.

The woman picked the bird out of Miss Mallory's palm and, as she took it in, her face began to glow, just a titch. It was the sort of glow Miss Mallory had seen thousands of times before.

The sort of glow a person got when she's found something she never knew she was searching for.

The glow of a perfect match.

"I haven't seen one of these in *years*," the woman said softly. She ran her fingers over the smooth contours of the bird's back. "My granny always used one of these, every time she made one of her blackberry pies. Baked it right inside with the filling, and the hot air funneled out the beak." She showed Miss Mallory the small round opening in the bird's yellow mouth. "Granny always said that was the secret to her flaky crust. How did you . . . ?"

Miss Mallory shrugged. "I just had a feeling it might belong with you."

As Miss Mallory picked her way through the bleachers to the spot that Toby had reserved beside him, she glanced over her shoulder just long enough to catch sight of Cady, stirring a dark batter with a pained look on her face. And as Miss Mallory did so, she felt yet another tug in her chest. It was a strong one this time, assertive and dogged, the same heart-yanking tug she'd been ignoring all week. For over a decade, really. And even if she thought she might have deciphered its meaning, Miss Mallory already knew that it was too late to do anything about it.

Cady had already found her perfect family and, for better or worse, it did not include Miss Mallory.

Mrs. Asher

IT DID NOT TAKE LONG TO GET TO NEW YORK CITY (SPEED limits, Dolores was certain, did not apply to women whose children had gone missing). Parking, however, was another matter. The closest spot Dolores could find was outside Grand Central Terminal, several long blocks from the convention center.

"It won't take you ten minutes to get there," a friendly stranger with an obvious Talent for applying blue eye shadow informed her. Dolores clutched Sally tighter to her chest. She could feel the ferret's tiny heart beating frantically beneath her fur. The poor creature must be missing Will something terrible. "Just get on the express bus at the corner and take it crosstown to—"

With no warning at all, Sally leapt from Dolores's arms. And before Dolores knew what was happening, she found herself chasing a ferret down the New York City sidewalk. "Sally!" she screeched as she ran. "Come back here!" Dolores would never forgive herself if she lost her son and his pet in the same afternoon.

Sally did not come back. She skittered and jumped, hopping from this pedestrian's shoulder to that hot dog vendor's cart. Dolores was close behind, scattering shopping bags and pigeons as she went. The creature scampered through a large glass revolving door studded with brasswork, and Dolores followed, through to the bustling hive of Grand Central Terminal's main room.

"*Sally!*"

Down the staircase, up another, around the bend, past the ticket booth Sally ran, and Dolores, too, huffing and puffing till she thought she couldn't run any farther. And then . . .

Wham!

Dolores smacked directly into her youngest son. He was cradling Sally in his arms, a stunned look on his face.

"Mom?"

"Will!" She swooped him up in a hug. "Where have you been? I've been searching *everywhere* for you."

Will jerked his head to the train behind him, where passengers were still climbing down the steps. "I was looking for Sally."

"How many times do I have to tell you to stay in one place

when you get lost, Willard Asher?" Dolores's words wanted to be stern, but the second hug she gave her son betrayed her happiness.

Trapped between them, Sally let out a *click-click-clack* of annoyance.

"I really would've rather you had a Talent for cheese-making, you know," Dolores went on, ignoring the ferret. "When we get home, I'm tying you to the doorknob."

"I'm sorry, Mom," Will said with a sniffle.

"I know you are, sweetie." She tousled his mop of brown curls. "What do you say we head on home?" When Will nodded, Dolores took his hand, squeezed it tight then tighter, and led him back through the station, while Sally tucked herself into her favorite spot around Will's neck. "Maybe from now on you could try to find adventures in books," Dolores suggested while they walked. "They have plenty, you know. Giants and monsters and cake. They're all right there, and you wouldn't even have to give your mother a heart attack to go on one." Will wrinkled his nose. "You don't like that idea?" she asked him.

"Haven't you ever had anything you loved doing, Mom?" Will replied. He reached up with his unsqueezed hand to scratch Sally's head. "Something that was worth getting in real big trouble for?"

For the first time in over an hour, Dolores's thoughts drifted to the ancient toe bone, worth millions of dollars, that she'd left sitting on the armrest of her car. Funny how something she'd treasured for over a decade could be so quickly forgotten. "Yes," she told her son. "I suppose I have."

When they reached the revolving door at the front of the station, Dolores stopped short.

"Mom?" Will asked, looking up at her. "What's the matter? Why'd you stop walking?"

Dolores's eyes flicked to the sign just outside on the sidewalk. BUS STOP.

"I hear it doesn't take ten minutes to get to the convention center," she told her son. "Wouldn't you like to see Cady win that bakeoff?"

At first, Will didn't seem to understand, but suddenly his eyes went wide. "Cake?" he asked.

Dolores grinned. "You might as well finish your adventure now that you've started it, huh?"

Will clapped his hands together and cheered. And—*click-click-clack!*—Sally seemed excited, too.

"After that," Dolores continued as they snaked their way out the door and through the crowds to the bus stop, "I have an adventure of my own to finish."

The Owner

IT WAS EASY ENOUGH TO PUSH PAST THE OVERSIZE WOMAN WITH the clipboard guarding the main doors. She was too busy gazing at some silly figurine to even notice him. And at last he spotted the girl, in the middle of the row of ovens. Wisp of a thing though she was, her crow-black hair gave her away. She was just pulling a cake off the rack. She set it on the counter, closing the oven door as the Owner made his way over to her. His feet hit the floor with every step.

Marigold

MARIGOLD SPOTTED IT BEFORE ZANE DID. AFTER SNEAKING through the delivery entrance, the two children had wiggled their way onto the main floor. Now they stood between the teeming crowds of people and the increasingly sensational cakes on display, searching for some way they might possibly be needed.

And Marigold spotted it.

There was Cady, at her oven, petite and wide-eyed and unsuspecting. Not fifty feet away was the Owner of the Emporium, approaching her rapidly, his gaze fixed.

"Zane!" Marigold screeched, searching for a path to push herself through to the baking stations. "Zane, we have to get over there!" Cady was one of the biggest-hearted people Marigold had ever met—she tried harder than anybody else to make others happy—and now the Owner was going to steal her Talent, just like he'd stolen Zane's. If Marigold had learned anything that week, it was that trying hard and being a good person didn't always mean that good things would happen to you.

But maybe it *did* mean that others might try on your behalf.

"We have to stop him!" she told Zane. "We have to help Cady." But there were so many people, and she and her brother were so far away. She yanked Zane past a greasy-haired young man powdered with flour. "What are we going to do?"

"Ow!" Zane shouted, suddenly wrenching to a halt. "My foot! Someone dropped a book on my foot." He picked it up.

"Zane, you moron, I don't care about some dumb book. We have to help Cady!" She tugged on his arm again.

They would never get there in time. Marigold's eyes scanned the room for another solution. There must be *something* that could stop the Owner. Her eyes landed on the fire alarm on the far wall, and the stringy, gray-haired woman nearby who seemed to be having a similar thought to Marigold's.

"It's V," Zane said.

Marigold nodded. "I know. I think she's going to pull the alarm."

"What?" Zane said. "No, I mean"—he held out the book to show her—"it's V. Look."

Marigold jerked her eyes from the figure across the room just long enough to glance at the book in Zane's hands. *Face Value.* There, underneath the words *Author Victoria Valence*, was a photo of V.

The woman without any words had written millions of them.

V

ALL HER LIFE, V HAD COUNTED ON HAVING HER WORDS
available to her whenever she needed to use them. She'd been
a master of words, that's what the reviewers had always said
about her. But, V thought as she spotted the red square of the
fire alarm, she might have found something even more useful.
If she could startle the chameleon just enough, he might show
his real face, and V might be able to foil any chameleon-like
schemes he'd been hatching.

Her thoughts turned again to the photograph she'd ripped
from the book.

The mother.

The father.

A baby girl.

V had been wrong before, thinking she saw Caroline in places she knew she wasn't. But the mother in that photograph—V would stake her life on it—was Caroline herself, clear as day. V had known her daughter in an instant, if only for the intricate twist of a braid she wore in her hair, the work of Talented fingers. And the baby . . .

Caroline had had a baby. She'd had a baby, and she hadn't even told her own mother. Tiny, wide-eyed, with a surprising amount of hair for an infant.

Nearing the fire alarm, V tapped her pocket for the reassuring feel of the photo and—with a gasp—discovered that it wasn't there. Nevertheless, she pressed on. She'd failed to communicate for years when she had the chance; she wasn't going to give up now.

Cady

CADY DID NOT EVEN NEED TO TASTE THE CAKE TO KNOW THAT it was not going to win her any trophies. She hadn't been able to decide what to make, and so she'd made a disaster. She'd created the whole mess in a daze, hoping for some flicker of inspiration. She'd dumped in the ingredients in a daze, clacked the wooden spoon through the bowl in a daze, and poured the tragic-looking batter into the pan in a daze. And inspiration had not come.

Apple caramel mocha poppy seed, that's what she'd ended up with. It certainly wasn't Cady's favorite. It wasn't *anybody's* favorite. She dropped the cake on the counter and yanked off her oven mitts. Cady had lost for sure, and now she'd let down Toby and Miss Mallory, too. She was as big a disaster as the mess in the pan, and all because she didn't know what kind of cake she'd like. She'd spent so many years wondering what other people might want that she'd never bothered to figure it out for herself. Suddenly, Cady felt like she didn't even know who she was.

Cady gazed down at the disastrous cake she'd just pulled from the oven. It didn't merely look unappetizing. It looked . . . unnatural. She sloped her nose nearer to the counter.

At the top of the cake, barely visible underneath a thin layer of crumbs, was a fist-size piece of paper. A photograph.

A woman.

A man.

A baby girl.

Cady brought her nose so close to the cake that she nearly nudged it. The woman had a braid, a beautifully elaborate one, trailing down her shoulder. And the baby—Cady blinked once, then twice—the baby girl had a braid as well. Cady was looking at a picture of herself. The woman with the braid must be her mother, and the man—with the crooked nose and the cowlicked hair—was her father.

Cady was so busy staring at the photograph, her mind swirling with questions, that she didn't hear the footsteps behind her until it was too late.

There was a sudden, icy spark at her forehead.

Toby

EVERY TIME THE MEMORY WEASELED ITS WAY BACK INSIDE Toby's brain, it stung, just as fiercely as though not a single day had passed. It twisted his stomach and made his cheeks burn. Caused his heart to shrivel and shrink inside him. Watching Miss Mallory now, the way she was examining her hands so closely to avoid watching Cady at her baking station, he remembered it all. And it stung.

"Please don't take her away from me," Toby said softly. "Please. If that's what you were going to say tonight. Please don't take Cady away. I don't . . . I don't think I could stand it."

Miss Mallory kept her gaze on her hands and said nothing.

Toby knew what it was to lose a child. That terrible day in Africa, just one week after his wife had died, he hadn't known. He couldn't have known how it would be, the guilt and the worry that he would suffer every day to follow. So he'd made the decision that he'd come to regret for the rest of his life. At the time, it had seemed wise. After all, what had he understood then about fatherhood? Absolutely nothing. Better his precious baby Cora grow up with new parents who could give her everything she wanted than with a half-wit like him. That's what he'd thought at the time.

Afterward, he'd run. Changed his face, changed his name. Taken the job he'd never wanted at the Emporium. But Toby had never forgiven himself.

Beside him, Miss Mallory cleared her throat quietly. "I won't take her away," she said, still studying her hands. "Even if I wanted to, I . . . You're the father she was meant to have. I can tell." She clutched her fist to her chest, as though a severe pain stung her there. "And all I want is for Cady to be happy."

Toby nodded at that, hope beginning to rise inside him once more. "I guess that's all we can ask for, isn't it?" he said slowly. "All we *should* ask for." He did want Cady to be happy. Cora, too—the daughter he'd never see again. Sometimes he found himself wondering what had happened to her after Dolores Asher had taken her to the orphanage that day in Madagascar. Had she found happiness, that tiny pixie of a girl with her beautiful braided hair? He hoped so. He hoped that, somewhere, she was half as happy as—

Down on the main exhibition area, there was Cady, just as she had been a moment before. But someone else was there, too.

The old man. His palm was pressed to Cady's forehead.

Toby leapt to his feet. "Stop!" he cried. It might be too late to help her, but he had to try anyway. That's what fathers were meant to do. "Dad! *Stop!*"

Zane

THERE WAS A PIERCING SQUEAL, AN ALARM, AND FROM THE ceiling the safety sprinklers sprung to life, showering water down the entire length of the floor. The crowd screeched and began bumping this way and that, all of them. It was chaos.

"Zane!" Marigold hollered at him. He turned his focus from the book to where his sister was pointing, across the room. He could just make them out through the screaming crowd and the gushing sprinklers. Cady was staring down at her cake, bewildered. And the Owner, with the icy stone of Talent poised to melt into his skin, was grinning. "We have to stop him!" Marigold cried. "We have to stop him, Zane! Oh, I wish I had the Talent to *do* something."

Zane turned to her, eyes wide. What was it the man in the gray suit had said, about shooting in a healthy direction?

"You do," he told her.

The Owner

THE OWNER DIDN'T NOTICE IT AS THE FIRST SPRAY OF THE sprinklers hit his skin, but the arc of spit that flew from across the room was so perfectly aimed that there was no way it *couldn't* have hit his hand.

Smack!

It knocked the icy stone of precious Talent to the floor.

The Owner dropped to his hands and knees, scrambling to retrieve it. But even as he grasped at the Talent, the spray from the sprinklers began to melt the stone, right before his eyes. A fine mist rose from the pale pebble, slowly at first, then faster and faster. And soon everything Mason Darlington Burgess had ever wanted slipped through his fingers and floated up into the air, where it spread like a fog throughout the entire wide room. The Owner screamed. He shouted. He wailed. But his cries were lost in the piercing screech of the fire alarm, and he knew it was useless.

He'd spent his whole life searching for one thing, and now it was gone.

Cady

As the sprinklers gushed down, Cady's gaze followed the curious mist, traveling up from the Owner on the floor to the crowd around her.

And then her eyes settled on one face in particular. The face of someone who was rushing her way. It was Toby.

And then it wasn't.

With every drop of water that landed on Toby's face, Cady noticed something new about him.

His upturned eyebrows.

His crooked nose.

His cowlicked hair.

Cady turned to the terrible cake she'd baked and ripped out the photograph that had found its way inside.

"Dad?" she breathed.

There was no doubt about it. The man standing before her was one and the same as the man in the photo. Cady's father.

Toby looked from Cady to the photograph, slowly seeming to understand, while from the slick floor the Owner let out a low moan. Toby wiped a soaking lock of hair from his forehead and blinked the droplets from his eyes. "I'm so sorry, Cady. I should've . . . I never meant . . ." He blinked again. "I'm so sorry. For everything. What can I do to make it up to you? Whatever you want, I'll do it."

Cady took in Toby's new face, from his unruly hair to his pointy chin. "I . . ." Her brain whirled slowly. Her forehead ached with a slight chill. What *did* she want? Cady looked around the soaking mess of a room. The screeching alarm, the panicked bakers, the sopping cakes. And then, Cady couldn't help it.

She laughed.

"I think I just want to go home," she said.

And Toby—with his imperfect, crooked-nosed face—offered her a real smile. "Whatever makes you happy," he told her.

Will

WHEN WILL AND HIS MOTHER FINALLY ENTERED THE convention center, there was rain indoors, and lots of it. Screaming, wailing, shrieking, too. A fine mist wound its way inside Will's nose, making him feel like—of all things—baking. It was chaos, that was for sure.

But Will didn't pay too much attention to any of it. With Sally snuggled tightly around his neck, he made his way through the rain to the biggest cake he'd ever seen—a fifty-layer-high masterpiece of sugary wonder. "Can I try some?" he asked, and the baker beside the cake, clutching his floppy wet chef's hat, merely shrugged.

"Sure, kid," the baker replied, surveying the mess around him. "Why not?"

And as Will and Sally leaned in for their first bites, Will couldn't help but grin.

It really had been an adventure.

One Month Later . . .

Epilogue

CADY STOOD ATOP A SHORT STACK OF POWDER BLUE SUITCASES behind the circular counter on the main floor of the Lost Luggage Emporium, tapping her toe. "That'll be"—*tap, tap, tap*—"fifty-seven fifty," she told the customer.

Across the counter, the customer smiled and dug into her wallet for the correct change. "A steal!" she said.

Business at the Lost Luggage Emporium had never been so good. Today the customers snaked almost out the door. There were probably many reasons for the store's success: its new management, for one thing. (All of the building's operations were now in Toby's hands, as sole heir to the property after the Owner had disappeared without a trace. There were rumors the old man had been sighted in New Mexico, but no one had tried very hard to track him down.) The building's new coat of paint had probably made a difference, too, as had the newly planted flower beds out front and the smartly placed advertisements in newspapers all over the tristate area. But Cady suspected that the credit for most of the business's recent prosperity lay with Miss Mallory. Cady could see her now, over by the sweaters, matching a lanky blond customer to the perfect green V-neck. It seemed Miss Mallory's Talent for matching extended well beyond orphans (although there were orphans occasionally, too, at the Emporium; they came and went faster than Cady could blink).

Not ten feet away, Will Asher tumbled out of an air vent and somersaulted to a stop. Sally, wrapped snugly around his neck, *click-click-clack*ed irritably as Will ducked under the countertop.

"Mom says I'm s'posed to take over for you so you can set up for the party," he told Cady.

Cady swept the last of her customer's change into the cash register and wiped her hands on her red knitted apron. "It's all yours," she replied.

At the front door, Cady found Mr. Asher, who was handing samples to customers as they headed to their cars. (The Ashers never had moved back into their twelfth-story apartment. "There's so much more room for Will to get lost here," Mrs. Asher was fond of saying. And Cady didn't so much mind the company.) "Care for some peanut butter?" Mr. Asher asked a passing customer, offering one of the two dozen tiny paper cups perched on the tray in his hand. "A sample, ma'am? Sure, take one for your son, too." He handed out another. "Hi there, Cady," he greeted her. "Here, try the new batch. I think they're almost ready to sell, what do you think?"

Cady took a sample of her own and squeezed out a taste. She'd had a vat-load of peanut butter in the past few weeks, but surprisingly, it seemed to get better every time she tried it. She let the peanut butter settle on her tongue. Velvety smooth and mouthwateringly delicious. It might not have been *quite* as good as the original Darlington stuff, but with Cady and Toby and Miss Mallory and V and the Ashers working together to create it, it was pretty amazing. (And why wouldn't it be? Every one of them had received a bit of Cady's Talent that evening at the bakeoff. Well, every one of them except Mr. Asher, who seemed pleased as punch to act as business manager.)

Cady returned the empty cup to Mr. Asher's tray. "I bet we'll sell them by the truckful," she declared. "Oh, and"—she dug into her pocket and produced a small square of candy, wrapped in orange wax paper—"Marigold told me you have a soft spot for orange nougat."

The grin on Mr. Asher's face as he took the candy was proof enough that Marigold had been telling the truth.

A gorgeous afternoon awaited Cady outside. Bright and green

and breezy. The perfect weather for an Adoption Day party. Cady straightened the corners of the polka-dot cloth on the picnic table, while beside her, V set up her music stand. V was growing astonishingly good at playing oboe—Marigold, it turned out, was quite the teacher. Cady suspected that Marigold's many years of Talent-hunting had taught her a thing or two about patience.

It was frustrating, sometimes, having a grandmother you desperately wanted to talk to, who couldn't talk back. But as soon as V set her fingers on the keys of the oboe and began to play, it was almost as though she *could* talk. When she played, Victoria Valence seemed to find a way to express herself. All the sadness she'd ever felt, all the happiness, everything—it was all there in her music. And Cady felt like she could understand her.

As Cady organized the various parts of the party—table, games, food—slowly the others came out to join her. Mr. Asher placed a sign in the front window—CLOSED FOR ADOPTION DAY PARTY—and the stream of customers reduced to a trickle. Cady plunked a handful of plastic forks into a polka-dot cup, while Mrs. Asher filled Toby in on recent developments at the museum—including her fifth authorship on the paper about the discovery of the infamous toe bone.

"Zane doesn't want anyone to know this part," Mrs. Asher said, her voice low—but not low enough that Cady couldn't overhear. "But it's really thanks to him that they let me come

back at all. He wrote a letter on my behalf. Said if anyone understood about mistakes, it was him, and I'd done wrong but that
didn't mean I was worthless." She dabbed at the corner of her
eye. "Can you believe? What a doll, that one."

Cady looked up just in time to catch the *doll* karate-chop one
of Marigold's spit bubbles across the parking lot.

"Cady!" Zane called when he noticed her gaze. The three
shiny silver beads on his red Talent bracelet caught a ray of sunlight. "You *have* to watch this! Mari and me came up with a new
trick. Look."

And before Cady had a chance to respond, Zane zipped
across the gravel on his skateboard, until he suddenly—*slap,
wham, splat!*—jumped off the board, jerked it over his head, and
whacked the perfect loopty-loop of spit that his sister had spat at
him across the grass.

"Perfect!" Marigold shouted with a giggle. "Cady, wasn't that
perfect?"

"Where's the cake?" Will asked, suddenly appearing at Cady's
elbow. "Mom said you made cake." *Click-click-clack*, Sally
agreed.

Cady had indeed made a cake. It had been difficult, at first,
figuring out the perfect kind of cake to bake for her own Adoption Day party. Because it was a hard thing to know exactly who
you were, especially if you'd gone and lost nearly all your Talent.
But Cady thought she'd figured it out in the end. She pointed

---

to the front door, where Miss Mallory was just bringing out the platter. "There it is," she told Will.

Wha-pop! went the door on its hinges. (There were still a few things about the place that needed fixing.)

Cady watched as Toby helped Miss Mallory place the cake on the table, nestled between the bed of petunias on the left and the pansies on the right. Scattered throughout both beds was a third type of flower, an impeccable mix of the two others. Miss Mallory had brought the new flower with her when she'd moved to the Emporium. "It took me a while to figure it out," she'd explained to Cady as they'd planted, "but it turns out there are some things in this world that can fit perfectly in more than one spot."

Yes, Cady thought, perhaps it had taken her a long time to have an Adoption Day party of her own, but in the end she'd found not one but two perfect parents—the person who'd been so concerned with her happiness eleven years ago that he'd changed his entire life to get it for her, and the person who'd been concerned with it every day since. Tobias Darlington Burgess (Cady loved him even more with his real name and his real face—crooked nose, cowlicked hair, and all) and Jennifer Mallory. Cady was adopting them both. And although they were three very different people, Cady couldn't help thinking that when they were woven together, they fit exactly right, like the three strands of hair that Cady's birth mother had once tied up so intricately.

———

As the first few lilting notes of V's oboe drifted into the air, Cady's eye caught a movement far down the length of Argyle Road. She might have thought it was a customer if the man hadn't been walking *away* from the Emporium.

A giant of a man, wearing a pressed gray suit.

As quietly as she could, Cady left her friends to sneak down the dirt road. She caught up with the man in time to see him turn the corner onto the main highway. But just before he disappeared from view, the man in the gray suit paused to stretch his leg into a bush. With the toe of his shoe, he nudged something out onto the dirt road. He turned to Cady, and he winked.

Then he was gone.

Cady scuttled to the bush and picked up the object. It was a jar, a small one, with the lid sealed tight. No label. It appeared to be empty, but Cady suspected that it might, perhaps, be a Talent, one of the Owner's that shattered in the road a month before.

Only this one hadn't.

Cady raised the jar above her nose, gazing at the emptiness. She could be holding a Talent for tightrope-walking, or making rocking chairs, or finding gold coins. Cady could open it right then and there and breathe it all up at once. Or she could give it to Zane, who was now nearly as Talentless as she was. Or she could smash it in the road and leave it for the squirrels.

Cady grinned a sideways sort of grin. She wasn't certain, but she thought perhaps it was a grin that suggested she knew more about the world than she was letting on. Because Cady seemed to remember a bit of advice she'd been given not so long ago.

It's the way we deal with what Fate hands us that defines who we are.

Cady tucked the jar inside her pocket. She'd have plenty of time to decide about things like that. Just at the moment, she had a cake to taste.

Cady's Chocolate-Almond-Cherry Cake

— a cake that perfectly braids together three very different flavors —

FOR THE CAKE:

  2 cups granulated sugar, separated

  ¼ cup unsweetened cocoa powder

  3 ½ cups flour (plus extra for preparing the cake pan)

  3 tsp baking powder

  ½ tsp salt

  1 cup butter (2 sticks), at room temperature
     (plus extra for greasing the cake pan)

  4 large eggs, at room temperature

  1 cup milk, at room temperature

  1 tsp almond extract

  1 tsp cherry extract

  ½ tsp red food coloring

1. Preheat oven to 350°F. Grease a 10-inch tube pan or Bundt pan with butter, and flour lightly.

2. In a small bowl, whisk together ½ cup of the sugar and all of the cocoa powder. Set aside.

3. In a medium bowl, whisk together the flour, baking powder, and salt. Set aside.

4. In a large bowl, cream the butter with an electric mixer on medium speed until smooth, about 2 minutes. Gradually add the remaining 1 ½ cups of sugar, beating until light and fluffy, about 2 to 3 minutes. Add the eggs, one at a time, beating well after each addition.

5. With the mixer on low speed, add about a third of the flour mixture to the butter mixture, combining well. Add about a half of the milk and combine. Then add another third of the flour mixture, the last of the milk, and then the last of the flour, combining well each time.

6. Divide the batter evenly between three clean medium bowls. Add the cocoa powder mixture to the batter in the first bowl, and combine thoroughly with a spoon or clean beaters. Spoon the batter into the bottom of the cake pan. Do not smooth down.

7. Add the almond extract to the batter in the second bowl, and combine thoroughly with a spoon or clean beaters. Spoon this batter over the chocolate batter already in the cake pan. Do not mix.

8. Add the cherry extract and red food coloring to the batter in the third bowl, and combine thoroughly with a spoon or clean beaters. Spoon this batter over the almond and chocolate batters already in the cake pan. Using a small spatula

or butter knife, cut through the layers of batter from one side of the pan to another, lifting slightly as you go, to create a marbled design. Do not overmix.

9. Bake for 1 hour, or until a toothpick comes out clean. Cool the cake completely before serving.

Turn the page for a sample of
the magical companion novel

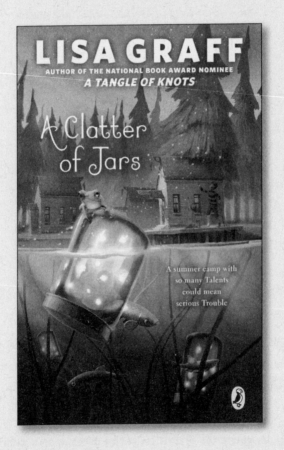

LISA GRAFF

AUTHOR OF THE NATIONAL BOOK AWARD NOMINEE
A TANGLE OF KNOTS

A Clatter
of Jars

A summer camp with
so many Talents
could mean
serious Trouble

Lily's Watermelon Limeade Float

———— a drink reminiscent of all the best birthday parties ————

FOR THE WATERMELON LIMEADE:
  4 cups chopped watermelon, from half of one small
    watermelon
  2 tbsp lime juice, from one lime
  1/2 cup sugar
  1 liter (4 cups) seltzer

FOR THE FLOAT:
  vanilla ice cream

1. In a blender or food processor, blend the watermelon, lime juice, sugar, and seltzer for just a few seconds, until smooth. Carefully pour through a wire-mesh strainer into a 2-quart pitcher. Discard the solids.

2. To serve, scoop ice cream into the bottom of a short glass. Pour the watermelon limeade over the top, and enjoy!

   [Serves 8]

Lily

LILY STOOD OUTSIDE THE DOOR TO THE INFIRMARY, winding the length of swampy green yarn around her right thumb. In every corner of the woods, campers were squealing, laughing, making friends, and generally kicking up a lot of dust. But Lily was focused on that length of yarn.

"Liliana Vera?"

In front of Lily stood a lanky counselor wearing a pine green Camp Atropos T-shirt, the name *Del* printed below the neckline.

"Are you Liliana?" Del asked. "I'm gathering Cabin Eight campers."

Lily glanced past Del to the flag circle, where four campers stood amid their luggage. "I'm Lily," she said.

"Great!" Del jerked his chin toward her duffel bag. "Need help with that?"

Lily shook her head, her wavy brown hair grazing her shoulders. "I got it," she said. Del looked skeptical, probably because Lily was hardly taller than the duffel was long. But Lily focused her thoughts at the bridge of her nose and, darting her eyes to the duffel, the bag rose—one inch, then five—off the ground. Lily took a step forward in the dirt, and the bag took a step with her.

"No need to ask what *your* Talent is," Del said, watching the bag drift forward. "Been a while since we had a Pinnacle here." Lily swelled with the smallest inkling of pride. "Welcome to Camp Atropos for Singular Talents, Liliana Vera. A haven for the most remarkable children in the world." As they neared the flag circle, Del pointed to each of the four campers, rattling off names. "Miles, Renny, Chuck, and Ellie." Lily did a double take when Del named the last two. Chuck and Ellie were identical twin girls. "Your bunkmates for the next two weeks. Let's get you all to Cabin Eight, shall we?"

"Hi!" Ellie greeted Lily as they began their trek though the woods. Lily could tell the twins apart because, despite having identical faces and identical dark brown skin, Ellie had a headful of teeny braids pulled into a ponytail and was wearing pale blue sneakers, while Chuck's hair was styled into wavy cornrows, and she wore Kelly-green high-tops. "Do you like frogs?" Ellie asked. "Chuck and I can identify any species."

"Uh," Lily replied. "Cool."

That's when one of the boys, Miles, piped up. "Singular Talents are understood as feats beyond standard human abilities and/or the laws of physics," he said. His voice was flat, his gaze fixed on the dirt in front of him as he walked.

"Huh?" Ellie asked.

"I think what he means," said the other boy, Renny, "is that identifying frogs isn't a Singular Talent. Either that or he just likes showing off how much of that textbook he memorized."

Beside her sister, Chuck snorted. "Oh, man," she said. "They're on to us now, Ellie. I guess we'll have to leave and go to regular person camp."

Ellie poked her twin in the side. "Chuck, *please*," she said.

They were deep in the shadows of the trees when Renny joined step beside Lily. He was tall and skinny, with pasty white legs. "Is this your brother?" Renny asked, his nose buried in a small photo book. He flipped a page. "Cute kid."

"Hey!" Lily cried, realizing what Renny was holding. "Give me that!" Focusing her thoughts at the bridge of her nose, she tugged the photo book toward her through the air. With her concentration no longer upon it, her duffel thunked to the dirt. The front pocket had been zipped open.

Lily inspected the album for damage, wiping away a smudge from the photo of Max's fifth birthday party three years earlier. It was one of Lily's favorites. Her little brother was balancing a plate of chocolate cake on his pinkie, his other arm wrapped around Lily. Lily, meanwhile, was using her own Talent to push the cake toward Max's nose. It was the last birthday she and Max had celebrated before their mother remarried and their step-sister, Hannah, buzzed into their lives like a housefly. Hannah had to go and be born the same day as Max—same year and everything—so in every birthday photo after that, it was Hannah that Max had his arm around.

At least Hannah had been assigned to a different cabin for the two weeks of camp, Lily reminded herself, zipping the photo book back in its pocket. She hoisted the duffel to her shoulder, which immediately ached in protest.

"You should keep a better eye on your stuff," Renny said. And when Lily scowled, he didn't even have the decency to look sorry. Instead, he stretched out his arm, like he wanted to shake hands. "Renwick Fennelbridge," he told her. "You might have heard of me."

Despite herself, Lily was impressed. She'd studied the Fennelbridges last year in her Singular Education elective, and she found them fascinating. Every family member was Singular, with some of the most fantastical Talents ever recorded.

"Can you really read minds?" she asked.

That's when the other boy, Miles, piped up again. "Renwick Chester Ulysses Fennelbridge," he said, his eyes still fixed on the dirt. "Eleven years old as of his last birthday. The only living Scanner, according to A *Singular History*. Fun fact: Renwick Fennelbridge was once flown to Rome, Italy, to read the mind of the pope, but got food poisoning on the plane and had to go home."

"*Please* find a new fun fact, Miles," Renny grumbled.

"You really know your Talent history, huh?" Lily said to Miles. Singular Education had been Lily's favorite class last year. Her teacher had been so impressed with her report on Ekers and Coaxes that she'd had Lily read it during the opening ceremony of the Talent festival. "Do you know about Evrim Boz?"

Miles responded without hesitation. "Evrim Biber Boz. Born 1576, died 1602. Talent: Coax. Able to wheedle Talents from one person to another and back again, even transferring Talents into inanimate objects to create Artifacts. Fun fact: The Talent Library in Munich, Germany, has eight of Evrim Boz's Artifacts on display, including a cooking pot that makes anything boiled inside taste like lentil stew."

"Did you know that later in her life, Evrim Boz said she wished she'd never created any Artifacts at all?" Lily asked, scurrying to keep up with him. Unlike Ekers, who could only steal Talents, Coaxes could pass Talents on—either to other people or to objects. "Because once you make an Artifact, you can't get the Talent back out. Evrim Boz tried once, with a pair of scissors that she'd Coaxed a beard-trimming Talent into, and instead she accidentally replaced the beard-trimming with her brother's Talent for cartography." Lily had always had a particular interest in Artifacts and the people who used them. "Evrim Boz's brother never spoke to her after that."

Miles didn't even glance at Lily before continuing his recitation. "Maevis Marion Marvallous. Sixty-seven years old as of her last birthday. Talent: Mimic. Able to duplicate the Talent of any person she comes in contact with for approximately one year."

"Now you've set him off," Renny muttered. "When Miles gets started on Talent history, good luck getting him to stop."

"Fun fact," Miles went on. "Maevis Marvallous alleges that she lost her Talent over three decades ago, although scholars debate the claim."

Suddenly Lily noticed that Miles and Renny had the same sharp nose. Same auburn hair. Same pasty knees. Miles was a bit broader, but they were brothers, no question.

"I didn't know there were two Fennelbridge kids," Lily said. She was sure *A Singular History* had mentioned only one. "What's his Talent?"

Renny halted midstride to tug at the top of his right sock. "Make enough Fennelbridges, and one of them's bound to be Fair." He let out a sour laugh. "That's what our dad likes to say."

"If you ask me," Chuck chimed in, "there are two Fair kids in the Fennelbridge family."

"What do you mean by that?" Renny snapped.

***

"You obviously stink at reading minds," Chuck informed him. "I've been mentally threatening to pop you in the jaw for the past ten minutes, and you haven't flinched once."

Lily couldn't help it. She laughed.

Oblivious to the awkwardness behind him, Del pointed to a sturdy building hewn from logs. "There's the lodge," he called back. "Meals are served on the mess deck. All-camp slumber party's the second Friday of camp, and the Talent show's that Sunday, before your parents take you home."

At the mention of the Talent show, Lily's heart snagged her chest. Maybe there was still time to come up with a new act to perform with Max.

A lot could happen in two weeks.

"The lodge also houses the office of our camp director, Jo," Del continued. "She plays a mean harmonica."

Miles broke from his Talent history just long enough to tell the dirt, "I play a nice harmonica. I learned last year in music. Cassandra Colby Donovan. Born 1851, died 1900. Talent: Quest. Fun fact: Cassandra Donovan was the Needle-in-a-Haystack champion of Baxley, Georgia, for forty years running, until they retired the competition."

"Up ahead is the archery ring," Del went on. "There's the fire pit, where we hold our campfire each Friday. And if you squint, you can make out the lake through the trees."

At that, Miles stopped walking. "No water!" he squeaked.

Del offered Miles a friendly smile. "What's wrong with a little"—he spit into one hand and pressed his palms together before sprinkling miniature icicles in the dirt—"*water?*" He took in Miles's alarmed expression. "Not a fan of a classic Numbing Talent, huh?" Del cleared his throat. The ice-spit at his feet was already melting in the sun. "Uh . . . canoes are available every day after breakfast, and if you feel like swimming, Jo encourages you to grab your towel any time of day and hop right in the water."

"*No water!*"

Miles shrieked it that time. And he began flicking his fingers, too—*flick-flick-flick-flick-flick!*

Quick as lightning, Renny grabbed his brother's hand. "You guys sell Caramel Crème bars at the camp store, right?" Renny asked Del. Miles's fingers slowly ceased their flicking. "Miles loves Caramel Crème bars."

"I want a Caramel Crème bar," Miles said, pulling his hand free. If Lily hadn't witnessed the scene herself, she'd never have believed that Miles had been in a near panic thirty seconds earlier.

"Uh . . ." Del scratched a spot below his ear. "What was the question again?"

"Caramel Crème bars," Renny reminded him.

"Oh. Right."

As Del went over the store's hours, Lily wound the length of yarn around her thumb, watching Renny with his brother. Lily had tied the yarn around her thumb three weeks ago. Since then, the lime green strands had turned swampy, thinning and separating, and the skin underneath had grown raw from constant rubbing. It had stung for some time, like a blister— insistent, sharp, painful. But Lily hadn't untied it.

She tugged her duffel farther up her aching shoulder, her attention stolen by the music drifting through one of the lodge's windows. It was a song Lily was quite familiar with. This was an instrumental version, without lyrics, but Lily knew the words by heart.

> *Los golpes en la vida*
> *preparan nuestros corazones*
> *como el fuego forja al acero.*

Lily and Max's father had sung them the melancholy lullaby countless times, on nights when he wasn't traveling for work. When he sang the tune, the notes swept you up and cradled you, made you feel safe.

("Why do you always have to travel?" Lily had asked him last year, when he'd been in Prague instead of her school auditorium for the opening ceremony of the Talent festival. He'd responded as he always did. Not that it was his job—not that he *had* to be away so often, that he had no choice—but rather: "Oh,

Liria. Traveling helps ease my heartache." Which didn't explain why her father had begun his travels long before he and Lily's mother had been married.)

Lily let the words of the song sink in. Her father had translated the lyrics for her once, but she never felt she truly understood them in any language.

> *The blows of life*
> *prepare our hearts*
> *like fire forges iron.*

Summer camp, Lily thought, pulling herself from the music to rejoin the tour, didn't seem like a place for melancholy songs.

When they reached Cabin Eight, Del creaked open the door and let them inside.

"Cordelia Fabius Sibson," Miles said as he entered the cabin. "Eighty-two years old as of her last birthday. Talent: Scribe."

Lily wound the length of yarn around her right thumb, staring at the three bunks that lined the cabin walls.

Three bunks.

Six beds.

"Are we waiting for another camper?" Chuck asked Del. "There are six beds, and only five of us."

"The assignments for this cabin were a little odd," Del

admitted. "I don't know what Jo was thinking, but you don't question Jo. Anyway, you were supposed to have one more cabinmate, but at the last minute, he—"

Lily dropped her duffel with a heavy *thunk*. "I need to go to the infirmary," she said.

"You okay?" Del asked, stitching his eyebrows together.

"I have to go," Lily repeated. And she squeezed past him out the door, racing down the path. Kicking up dirt.

It should have been Max in that sixth bed. It should have been their summer together, while Hannah the housefly was far off in a different cabin, buzzing at someone else. But they weren't together, because three weeks ago, Max had gotten hurt.

Around and around went the length of yarn.

Lily was the one who'd hurt him.

Turn the page for a sample of

FAR AWAY,

a poignant, heartfelt novel by Lisa Graff.

PROLOGUE

PEOPLE ALWAYS TRY to feel sorry for me when they find out my mom died, but I like to look on the bright side. Like, she never stops me from eating extra cookies, or forces me to study when I don't want to. She's never scolded me for staying up past my bedtime, either—although she usually tells Aunt Nic to scold me later.

"Where is she right now?" I used to ask Aunt Nic. I asked that practically once an hour when I was a little kid. "She hasn't been drawn Far Away, has she?" I was terrified of the idea of my mother going Far Away for good, like my grandparents had before I was born. Once a spirit takes up permanent residence Far Away, it's nearly impossible to communicate with them anymore, and I like to talk to my mom as much as I can.

But Aunt Nic would assure me every time.

"Don't worry, CJ," she'd say. "She's still here on Earth, keeping an eye on you—and she's Far Away, too, with Grandma and Grandpa Ames and all the other spirits. She's in both places at the same time."

But I would never feel *really* satisfied until my mother told me herself. She usually did that at night, after dinner, while I was sitting in a folding chair scooched up against our motor home's kitchen sink and Aunt Nic was massaging shampoo into my curls under the just-right warm water.

"I'm right here, CJ, darling," she would say. It was always Aunt Nic's voice, of course, but the words were my mom's. You can tell when Aunt Nic's talking to Spirit, because her words get softer, slower, like she's listening at the same time she's talking. I may have been dealt a bad hand, being born to a mom who was going to die four hours later, but at least I got lucky enough to have an aunt who could communicate with her. A "medium," that's what most folks call her—because Aunt Nic can deliver messages from both sides.

"But *where* are you?" I asked my mom once. "I mean, *exactly.*" It was my fifth birthday—I remember, because Aunt Nic was taking ages washing my hair, and I was wondering if we were ever going to get to birthday cake. "Are you sitting on the couch?" Our motor home, back then, had an ugly brown corduroy couch that was our seat for the table, and my bed, too. "Are you swimming in the sink?"

"Sweet seedling," my mom replied. I always love when she calls me "seedling." It makes me feel warm, like being wrapped up in a blanket. *"I'm everywhere and nowhere all at once."*

And I guess that answer must've done it for me, because I

pulled my head out of the sink to ask an even more important question.

"Can you tell Aunt Nic I'm ready for my birthday cake?"

My mom just laughed, right through Aunt Nic. *"I helped your aunt find something even better this year,"* she told me as Aunt Nic squeezed the water out of my curls. The shower in our motor home was nearly as busted as the engine, so Aunt Nic washed my hair in the sink every night and helped me work cream through it after so the curls stayed bouncy.

"Nothing's better than birthday cake," I told my mom and my aunt together.

I guess they didn't agree, because Aunt Nic only wrapped a towel snug around my hair and walked over to the motor home fridge. I watched as she poked around the leftover rice and macaroni salad, and the ketchup bottle that had tipped over so many times the rim was red with goo. Finally she pulled out two tiny Styrofoam containers and set them on the table in front of the couch. I came over to see.

When Aunt Nic peeled the lid off the first container, I wrinkled my nose right up on my face. Light brown glop with curved dark sprinkles—that's what my mom and Aunt Nic had gotten me instead of birthday cake. I was about to say it didn't look like anything I wanted to eat when my mom started in with one of her stories.

"I was young when you were born," she said, and I could tell

right away that this was a story I was going to want to listen to. *"Just nearly twenty."*

Aunt Nic jumped in then, only she didn't say anything to me. She started talking directly to my mom. That happened sometimes.

"Yes, Jennie June," Aunt Nic said. "'Young *and* gorgeous.' I was gonna add that part."

I tucked my feet under my butt to get comfortable.

"I was excited to meet you," my mom went on, *"but I'm not gonna pretend I had my act together. For one thing, I'd lost track of your dad before he was lucky enough to know he was having a daughter."*

My mom and Aunt Nic always say that I'm the product of a "whirlwind romance"—but I never figure I miss out much, not having a dad. Two grown-ups who care about you is as much as most kids get.

"And then the morning of December sixth came," my mom said, *"and I hadn't even picked out a name for you yet, but it was clear you were coming, and quick."*

Aunt Nic raised her eyebrows at me then. "CJ," she said, "your mom wants me to tell you she was cool as a cucumber the whole time at the hospital, but—Jennie June, I'm not gonna lie to the girl. I was there!" When Aunt Nic's eyes went wide, I could tell my mom had words for her. "Well!" Aunt Nic chirped. "I'm not gonna repeat *that*."

"What happened after I was born?" I asked, to remind

them to keep going with the story. I had a feeling the next part was important.

"What happened, my seedling, was that you were gorgeous." My mom gave me a look then, through Aunt Nic, like the image had stayed with her, even though her body hadn't. *"Tiniest thing I'd ever seen, with dark, thick curls. And that birthmark!"* Through Aunt Nic, she reached out and pressed one thumb soft against my cheek, to the dark heart-shaped spot. *"That's called a 'cherish,' you know, that sort of mark."*

When I put my own hand to the spot, I could feel the memory of my mom's touch there, warm and gentle. I kept my hand like that for a long time.

"As soon as we were alone in the room," my mom continued, *"just us three Ames ladies—well, your aunt pulls a cooler out of her purse."*

"A cooler?" I asked.

"She'd brought it with her to the hospital! Had it on her the whole time, only I hadn't noticed."

Aunt Nic tilted her head to respond. "You were busy, Jennie June," she said.

"True," my mom replied.

"What was in the cooler?" I asked. Because sometimes they'd get so busy talking to each other they'd forget anyone else was listening.

It was Aunt Nic who answered that one. "Back where

Grandma Ames's family came from, in Lebanon," she said, peeling back the lid of the second Styrofoam cup, "whenever a new baby comes into the world, they serve caraway pudding. For good luck."

Peering down into that little white cup, I felt like I might be starting to understand. Those dark skinny curls on top of the pudding, I realized, were caraway seeds. Suddenly it didn't look so disgusting after all. My mom picked up the story as I dipped the tip of my spoon into the container.

"It only took a single bite of that pudding," she said, *"for me to know. I looked at you, tiny thing curled in my arms like a seed, and I told your aunt, 'Her name is Caraway.'"*

Maybe I'd heard the story before. But that day, on my fifth birthday, was the first time I remembered. It was definitely the day I realized that caraway pudding tasted a whole lot better than it looked. It became a tradition after that. Every year on my birthday, no matter what city we happen to be in, no matter how busy Aunt Nic is, my mom helps her track down some caraway pudding, and the three of us celebrate together. Even after Aunt Nic got to be "big potatoes" on the psychic medium circuit, and she hired Oscar and Cyrus to travel with us for extra help, and we swapped our busted motor home for the new tour bus with the fancy shower so I didn't need help washing my hair in the sink anymore—even after all that, Aunt Nic and my mom find time and pudding for my birthday. Every year.

I still remember the way that first bite tasted on my tongue, sweet and silky, as they told me the rest of the story. They left in every detail, even the ones so sad they made my throat tight with tears.

Like how, just minutes after she gave me my name, the hospital machines started beeping out of control and the nurses rushed in all panicked.

And how they tried and tried and tried to save her.

And—throat-clenchingest of all—how she died, right there in the bed beside me, from a sickness no one had known to look for.

But they told me the happy details, too.

Like how she visited Aunt Nic just days after she died, because she knew her sister had the Gift and could hear her when she spoke.

How she told Aunt Nic to be my guardian here on Earth while she cared for me in Spirit.

And how, since she'd left the world before giving me a middle name, my mom asked Aunt Nic to pick it.

"*You* picked June?" I asked Aunt Nic. "After my mom?"

Aunt Nic nodded. "Caraway June. 'Cause you're my sunshine in December."

The story was so filling—sweet like pudding, but with some bite to it, too—that it wasn't till I was scraping the last of my birthday dessert out of its cup that I thought to ask.

"Mom?" I said, touching the heart shape on the softest part of my cheek. "Why's it called a 'cherish'?"

My mom was quiet at first, and for a second I worried that she really had been drawn Far Away. But then Aunt Nic reached out across the ugly corduroy couch and gently unwrapped the towel from my hair. Eased my curls down to my shoulders. Picked up the hair cream and began working it through my hair, just like she did every night.

"Because you are so loved, CJ Ames," she told me as she coaxed my curls into perfect spirals, "so cherished, that it shows up on your very skin."

The funny thing was, I asked my mom the question, but it was my aunt who answered. But I guess I liked what she said too much to ask why.

Find out more about

LISA GRAFF's

other novels!

Ten kids,
a bunch of angry parents,
and one great war.

When Winnie's parents get divorced, her frustration at their constant fighting starts to grow until it's as big as a tree itself. By the end of fifth grade, she decides the only way to change things is to barricade herself in her treehouse until her parents come to their senses—and her friends decide to join her. It's kids versus grownups, and no one wants to back down first. But with ten kids in one treehouse, all with their own demands, Winnie discovers that things can get complicated pretty fast!

**A touching story about a boy
who won't let one tragic accident define him.**

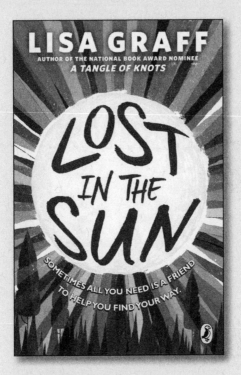

All Trent did was shoot a hockey puck, but that one little shot led to an unintended tragedy. Middle school could be his chance at a fresh start. Maybe he'll blend in. Maybe all will be forgotten. Maybe he can even join the baseball team. But none of that seems likely. Then he meets Fallon Little—the girl with the mysterious scar across her face—and starts to realize that everyone has their secrets, and it might just be possible, after all, to start over.

Albie has always been an almost.
He's almost good at tetherball.
He's almost smart enough to pass his spelling test.
He almost makes his parents proud.

And now that Albie is starting a brand-new school for fifth grade, he's never felt more certain that almost simply isn't good enough. With everyone around him expecting him to be one thing or another, how is an almost like Albie ever supposed to figure out who he really wants to be?

How far would you go to get something you really wanted?
Would you lick a lizard?
Wear a tutu to school?
Dye your hair green?

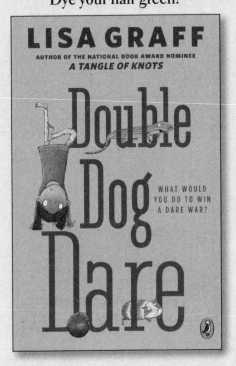

New kid Kansas Bloom (self-proclaimed King of Dares) and Media Club maven Francine Halata face off in a crazy Dare War to determine the future news anchor for the fourth-grade media club (a gig Francine has been dying to get forever). In a battle of wits and willpower, Francine and Kansas become fast enemies . . . until they discover that they have something surprising in common. And somehow, that one little fact changes everything.

A humorous story full of heart, courage, and a touch of magic.

Bernetta's summer couldn't be going any worse. First her ex–best friend frames her for starting a cheating ring in their private school, which causes Bernetta to lose her scholarship for seventh grade. Even worse, Bernetta's parents don't believe she's innocent and forbid her from performing at her father's magic club. Now Bernetta must take immediate action if she hopes to raise $9,000 for tuition. But that's a near impossible task with only three months until school. Enter Gabe, a boy con artist who's willing to team up with Bernetta to raise the money. But only if she's willing to use her talent for magic to scheme her way to success.